Twelve military heroes.
Twelve indomitable heroines.
One **UNIFORMLY HOT!** *miniseries.*

Don't miss Harlequin Blaze's first 12-book
continuity series, featuring irresistible soldiers
from all branches of the armed forces.

Watch for:

A FEW GOOD MEN by Tori Carrington
(Marines)
January 2009

ABLE-BODIED by Karen Foley
(Delta Force)
February 2009

ALWAYS READY by Joanne Rock
(Coast Guard)
March 2009

THE RIGHT STUFF by Lori Wilde
(Medical Corps)
April 2009

AFTERBURN by Kira Sinclair
(Air Force)
May 2009

LETTERS FROM HOME by Rhonda Nelson
(Army Rangers)
June 2009

Uniformly Hot!
The Few. The Proud. The Sexy as Hell.

Blaze

Dear Reader,

I've had the pleasure of working closely with military romance author Catherine Mann for years, reading all of her air force heroes before they'd go to print, as part of our critique partner relationship. Her WINGMEN WARRIORS characters inspire me with their call to serve and their dedication to duty. So when my editor wanted to bring a military series to Harlequin Blaze, I couldn't raise my hand quickly enough for the chance to create the kind of strong, committed hero I've seen Catherine pen—but with my very own Blaze twist!

Welcome to the third installment in the UNIFORMLY HOT! miniseries. I set the story in Puerto Rico after being inspired by a trip to this gorgeous island last year. I hope you enjoy the armchair vacation contained in this book along with Damon and Lacey's story. Please do e-mail me if you'd like to share your impressions of the book! It's always a pleasure to hear from readers at joanne@joannerock.com.

Happy reading,

Joanne Rock

Always Ready

JOANNE ROCK

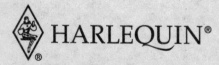

TORONTO • NEW YORK • LONDON
AMSTERDAM • PARIS • SYDNEY • HAMBURG
STOCKHOLM • ATHENS • TOKYO • MILAN • MADRID
PRAGUE • WARSAW • BUDAPEST • AUCKLAND

Recycling programs
for this product may
not exist in your area.

ISBN-13: 978-0-373-79461-4
ISBN-10:   0-373-79461-4

ALWAYS READY

www.eHarlequin.com

Printed in U.S.A.

ABOUT THE AUTHOR

Three-time RITA® Award nominee and Golden Heart winner Joanne Rock is the author of more than thirty books for Harlequin. Her matchmaker heroine was inspired by her own fascination with what draws people together. Like Lacey Sutherland, Joanne has fun studying Myers-Briggs profiles, astrology charts, Enneagrams and the occasional personal ad to help understand the esoteric component of couple chemistry. Whether she is writing a medieval historical or a sexy contemporary story, she enjoys exploring the dynamics that create a lasting relationship. Learn more about Joanne and her work by visiting her at: joannerock.com or at myspace.com/joanne_rock.

Books by Joanne Rock

HARLEQUIN BLAZE
135—GIRL GONE WILD*
139—DATE WITH A DIVA*
171—SILK CONFESSIONS**
182—HIS WICKED WAYS**
240—UP ALL NIGHT
256—HIDDEN OBSESSION†
305—DON'T LOOK BACK‡
311—JUST ONE LOOK‡
363—A BLAZING LITTLE CHRISTMAS
    "HIS FOR THE HOLIDAYS"
381—GETTING LUCKY
395—UP CLOSE AND PERSONAL
450—SHE THINKS HER EX IS SEXY...

HARLEQUIN HISTORICAL
749—THE BETROTHAL
    "HIGHLAND HANDFAST"
758—MY LADY'S FAVOR
769—THE LAIRD'S LADY
812—THE KNIGHT'S COURTSHIP
890—A KNIGHT MOST WICKED

*Single in South Beach
**West Side Confidential
†Perfect Timing
‡Night Eyes

To my critique partner, the inimitable Catherine Mann, who inspires me daily with her natural talent, her amazing work ethic, her commitment to her craft and—quite awesomely—her commitment to mine, as well. Thank you so much for the years of guidance and support!

1

A Private Island off the Florida Coast

You wouldn't recognize a good time if it landed in your lap and wiggled.

LACEY SUTHERLAND stared at the instant message from her twin sister—her fraternal, *meaner* twin, who had nothing in common with her besides a last name and a career path—and felt her blood boil.

It was long past midnight. Her latest blog on the matchmaking Web site she'd worked so hard to develop had received only a couple of hundred hits. Her career was in the crapper and had been headed there for months. Once, twice, again she thunked her forehead against her kitchen table that doubled as a work station. Her research manuals and computer printouts of reference material were piled under her chair, all over her countertops and stuffed in the nearby plate rack that made a really creative filing system. And now her ever-helpful twin who thought she knew best because she'd pushed her way out of the womb two minutes before Lacey wanted to tell her how to have a good time?

Rubbing her now sore head, she wondered if anyone

had popularized GTH as an e-mail acronym. Go to…
Hades fit Lacey's response quite aptly.

I don't need a vacation! Lacey typed back, picturing her twin on the other side of the country.

Laura lived in Seattle, a good three thousand miles away from Lacey's small plot of dirt just east of Miami off Florida's coast. Lacey had come by her own little island in the Atlantic thanks to a brilliant real-estate agent and a small windfall from the damages on a court case that she didn't like to remember. She was very content to be far from her roots and the sister who thought she knew everything from which wine to pour with a cheeseburger to what men Lacey should date.

Like now. Lacey's eyes went straight to the vacation brochure glaring at her from beside her computer. Laura had won a free airline ticket to anywhere in the U.S. and was convinced Lacey had to take it. She'd been on her soapbox about Lacey working too hard, when it was Laura's fault that her career was in shambles in the first place. Why her twin had to follow her into the matchmaking business after Lacey had declared an interest in the field was anyone's guess.

Some people took that "I can do anything better than you" mentality a little too far.

You haven't been off that damn speck of dirt you call an island in months. Her sister typed back, the instant message tone chiming.

It's bad enough you don't get nearly enough fresh foods out there, but you're turning into a hermit. Social skills disappear if you don't use them, darling.

Lacey rolled her eyes at the use of the endearment and the chain of smiley-faced emoticons that followed. Too bad there wasn't an emoticon for smugness.

Laura did strike a sore spot with the bit about Lacey's social skills, however. Lacey had reason to be antisocial after a traumatic incident when she'd been an overweight teen. That made her cautious. Appreciative of her privacy. And pretty damn picky when it came to dating.

That was why she'd gotten into matchmaking. She liked the idea that she could prescreen candidates— both for herself and for other discriminating singles.

I was in Miami six weeks ago and stocked up. She had enough Lean Cuisine suppers to go another six days without leaving her place, but she wasn't about to confess that to her hippie, fresh-veggie-loving sis. You're just scared I'm going to beat you in this contest and you can't wait to distract me from the goal.

After Lacey had majored in sociology, she'd worked in the matchmaking industry for a few years before taking a gamble and developing her own online dating Web site. She'd put a simple system in place that predicted compatibility to help serious daters find intelligent relationship prospects. Her program, Connections, had the highest rate of dating success stories for an independent matchmaker on the Web—until her sister had developed a competing site.

The Blender was an irreverent spin on dating services, focusing on fun matches instead of serious life partners, and had increasingly undermined Lacey's online traffic for nearly six months in a row. Finally, deciding to face the competition head-on, Lacey had promised her advertisers that this month her site would generate more hits than her sister's Web site, and more successful dates. The event would make or break Connections for good.

You're far more concerned about your numbers than me came Laura's speedy reply, the crisp, typed letters blinking back at Lacey.

Damn straight.

Her Web site was on the line, since she was losing major dollars to her sister's site.

A loss would not only crush her career, but could easily necessitate she give up her private haven in the middle of nowhere. Life out on the island wasn't cheap, but she dearly loved the quiet beauty that was so different from the noisy household she'd grown up in with her mother's endless parade of significant others. Or, in her mom's case, *in*significant others.

Cut the crap, Laura.

One in the morning was too late for diplomacy, Lacey decided, typing away with tired fingers.

If you're afraid of the competition, find another field.

She was about to close her instant-messenger window to end the conversation and plot her next step to create a big splash on her matchmaking blog, but her sister's newest note was already popping open.

The e-ticket for the flight to anywhere is already in your inbox. I can't take any trips right now since Brillo hates to fly.

The note was immediately followed by the tone that indicated Laura had signed off, ensuring her twin had the last word. As per usual.

And wasn't it amusing that Laura thought Lacey was a hermit with no social skills, yet Laura wouldn't fly because her *poodle* didn't like it? Dear God, what if she was like her sister in more ways than she realized?

Suddenly tempted by that plane ticket, if only to prove she hadn't turned antisocial in the years since college, Lacey allowed her mouse to hover over the icon for her e-mail inbox and then yanked it away. She refused to get sucked into her sister's Dr. Phil act. Laura loved to prescribe other people's life paths. That's what made her site so popular. Some people needed direction in life.

Lacey was not one of them.

Instead she clicked on the beta version of her new secret weapon—an updated matchmaking program that she'd been working on for the past six weeks she'd been holed up at home. She had hoped to get the system to market and start reaping the benefits before her month was up for this contest. Before she lost her top advertisers to Laura.

Before Lacey became the also-ran in her twin's six-foot-tall shadow. But glitches kept popping up in the program, discouraging her from introducing it to her site's visitors until she'd perfected it.

Lacey had been testing the new system by filling out her own matchmaking profile in the Connections database. Not that she was looking for a relationship right now.

Far from it.

Her work monopolized her life and probably would continue to do so for the next few years. Even if Connections shut down she wanted to be secure in her world and her career before she began searching for someone to share her life with. But she needed to try out the new system, and that meant going on a few sample dates to see what sorts of guys the process netted.

"Eat your heart out, sis." Lacey clicked on the "Match" function to see what kinds of mates her program had paired her with after her last round of software adjustments.

Excited all over again, Lacey sat up straighter in her ergonomic office chair pulled up to the kitchen table slash desk. She toasted the laptop screen with a coffee mug filled with sludge that had gone cold about two hours ago.

Bing.

An electronic ring told her the process was complete. Her matches had been run. Setting aside the chipped mug of high-octane caffeine, Lacey shoved her glasses higher on her nose to view the results.

At which time, her socks were promptly knocked off.

Because she hadn't received a batch of twenty crappy matches with seventy-five percent compatibility ratings. She'd scored two matches in the eighties along with the brass ring of the matchmaking world.

A ninety-six percenter.

She hardly dared to click on the profile that came with a hell of a lot of professional joy and—amazingly—a smidgen of romantic curiosity. What kind of guy rated so high that he would be ninety-six percent compatible with her?

Tapping the keys that would give her more information on one Nicholas Castine, Lacey read all the right things. College educated. Thirty-five years old, which meant he was over those party years and ready for something more serious. A real job as an importer-exporter. He owned his business, in fact.

Impressed, Lacey was already picturing herself meeting this guy. If not for her own dating pleasure, then for the sake of the blog during this all-important month when visitor traffic was crucial. She could chronicle the success of a ninety-six-percent match firsthand on the Connections site, a feature sure to generate interest in the new program if she had indeed smoothed out the last of the kinks.

Delirious with this renewed affirmation that she didn't suck as a matchmaker, Lacy was ready to click on the man's e-mail address and introduce herself. Then she spotted his current location.

Originally from New York City, Nicholas Castine had posted his profile last month from his second home in Aquadilla, Puerto Rico. A far-flung locale that would make for an ideal vacation, should a woman be so inclined. Maybe that bit of kismet was telling her that every once in a while a woman needed to believe in love. Fate.

The couple that was destined to be together.

Near Borinquen USCG Air Station
Puerto Rico
Five days later

THE NIGHT TOOK a downward turn the moment a hot chick stepped into the bar.

Coast Guard Lieutenant Damon Craig tipped back his glass of local rum and determined he could pinpoint the exact second his evening had gone from bad to worse. And it wasn't just because the woman in question carried a cell phone in one hand and a laptop satchel in the other for a drink at a beach surf-shack. Damon considered these hallmarks of self-important tourists his personal pet peeves during a night out.

No, the woman teetering around in expensive heels at Café Rosita's proved a problem because she was flirting with the object of Damon's current mission. With a delectable set of curves drawing the attention of every Y-chromosome holder in the bar, the woman made it damn difficult for Damon to keep tabs on his quarry.

And he needed to watch the drug runner. Damon might have entered the bar to blow off steam after a frustrating week of coming up with nothing on the drug shipment his unit in the USCG's Deployable Operations Group had been tasked to intercept. But then he'd spotted the reputed ringleader himself and decided to stick around and monitor the guy. If their intel about Nicholas Castine was right, he wasn't just importing Ecstasy and date-rape drugs, he was also a predator himself. One of many reasons Damon wasn't crazy about the cupcake in a yellow sundress chatting up the dirtbag.

"I could go over there," Damon's buddy across the table offered. Enrique Soto was a Puerto Rico native even though he'd gone to Coast Guard Academy in Connecticut with Damon back in the day. Another member of Damon's unit, Enrique was deployed with him at the Borinquen Air Station nearby. A big guy with a personality as loud as his Hawaiian shirt, Enrique wasn't the sort of dude people forgot—a fact that made good cover for Damon's impromptu mission tonight.

No one tended to notice Damon when Enrique jumped

behind the bar to show the locals his favorite rum concoctions or leaped on a table to start a round of Elvis karaoke.

The live band's mix of reggaeton and American pop hits filled the small café, vibrating along the rafters and rattling the glasses hanging upside down over the bar.

"And what do you think that will accomplish?" Damon set aside his empty glass, content to stretch out his drink orders even though he wasn't officially on duty. He would have forgone the rum altogether except that two Coasties sliding into a bar booth without slamming a drink or two would have the locals talking in no time. That was another reason Damon had chosen Enrique for company.

Enrique's nights off involved enough rum consumption for both of them.

"I'll charm the broad to get her out of the way so you can keep tabs on our guy. Your guy, technically, since I'm off tonight." Enrique picked up Damon's empty glass and waved it around as he whistled for the waitress. "Oh, that's right. You are, too. You just forgot how to stop working for more than five minutes at a time."

Clearly the guy's fifth rum wasn't mellowing him one damn bit.

"What makes you think I'm not here to get laid? That woman in the yellow sundress is right up my alley." Damon paid the waitress for the next round and kept his eyes on the hot chick and his drug-runner target, who seemed to be having some kind of tiff.

Damon didn't have a clear view since four other guys took turns checking out her legs and continually got in his way. But it looked like the woman had tensed, her tall, curvy form straightening in her seat beside Nick Castine.

After eight years in the Coast Guard, Damon had been in prime position for duty with the Deployable Operations Group. He liked the unit that allowed him to go anywhere in the U.S. at any given moment to respond quickly to new security threats. But this mission was about more than a job. The DOG's pursuit of Nicholas Castine meant the chance for vengeance on a man whose crime network had infiltrated Damon's personal life. Castine's drugs and the party lifestyle they encouraged had stolen Damon's last girlfriend right out from under him last year.

"Because you swore off women a year ago the first and only time I saw you get shit-faced." Enrique turned around to follow Damon's gaze. "And if I remember correctly, you specifically swore off sophisticated city women who thought they were better than the general population." He swung back to face Damon, a big grin on his mug. "I'd say the toots with the designer laptop case fits the bill."

Damon heard him in a peripheral sense, but couldn't quite tear his attention from the uptown girl who was now clearly trying to shove Castine off her. Was she a business associate? A new girlfriend intel didn't know about? For all Damon knew, she could be in the drug business. A buyer. A user. The dude's meaty hands had wrapped around her waist to drag her close, and she seemed to be putting a hell of a lot of effort into keeping him at bay. Muscles in her biceps and triceps flexed, her hands were splayed on the guy's chest, fingers bent back at an awkward angle at his forward momentum.

Yeah, the night was definitely taking a downward spiral. He wanted to watch this Castine guy and personally arrest his ass for providing half the U.S. with Ecstasy, Ketamine and Rohypnol, the so-called party drugs that tantalized good people into thinking happiness could be found in a drug-popping club or in a stranger's bed. Memories of his former girlfriend still burned his gut. In theory, it was no surprise that crimes carried out over international waters would finally affect Damon personally, since he'd been stationed at all the hot spots for drug and weapons importers over the course of his career. That's what being in the Coast Guard meant. But he'd still been stunned when the woman he was living with got hooked on the same drugs he'd been fighting to keep out of the U.S.

What this chick in the lemon-colored dress needed was one of those four guys who'd been gawking at her legs to get off his lazy ass and help her away from the overeager Romeo. Whether she was involved in Castine's business or not, she didn't deserve the manhandling. But it seemed every last one of the gawkers just watched in salacious envy as the creep wearing Gucci shades in a dark bar continued to grope her.

"Shit." Tension coiled inside him. Tighter.

Enrique turned. A waitress tried to intervene. And then Damon was on his feet, not caring if he blew his anonymity in front of a guy his group was investigating. People who took advantage of women were on his personal list of World's Biggest Jerk-offs.

Ten strides brought him tableside with Castine and the woman.

He lowered himself to eye level with the prick's sunglasses as the guy leaned back to laugh at his companion's Twister maneuvers.

"Didn't anyone ever tell you that 'no' means 'no'?"

Damon counted on a surprise tactic and created a path for the lady to clear out of the booth.

He held his hand out to help her up as Castine loosened his hold.

"We were just getting better acquainted, weren't we, Lacey?" The reputed drug runner straightened his suit jacket and smoothed a pink silk tie as he looked to his reluctant date for confirmation.

She stood quickly, tugging her purse and her laptop case out from under the table.

"Actually, you were just demonstrating what a low-life you are." She spoke English with a distinctively American accent and gave a cold nod to the jackass who'd tried to maul her. Then she spun toward Damon. "Thank you."

With a fluff of her short blond curls, she pivoted on her heel and swished past him, her yellow skirt brushing his knee as she went.

Half the heads in the bar turned in unison to watch her go, and he knew he couldn't let her wander around this deserted stretch of Aquadilla on her own when she was so obviously out of her element. She could spend half the night trying to talk a cab driver into taking her back to the more tourist-friendly part of town. If the cabbies on duty around here were half as interested in her legs as the bar patrons had been, she'd be fighting an uphill battle.

"Looks like she's already gotten acquainted enough," Damon observed as he walked away from Castine's table.

He'd already hit the bottom of the evening downward spiral by making his quarry aware of his presence. Not even a hot chick with a bad attitude could make this night worse.

"CAN YOU TAKE ME to this hotel?"

Lacey Sutherland handed the address to a cab driver who was leaning on his trunk, desperate to get out of the seedy bar scene and back to her luxury hotel for the night.

She liked Puerto Rico, but she hadn't found her bearings yet and had somehow misjudged the bar's proximity to the resort. Staying out on the northwestern shore was nothing like metropolitan San Juan, where she'd spent the first night after her plane touched down.

She didn't even want to think about how horribly she'd misjudged her date. That was a problem on so many more levels than it would be for a normal woman, since Lacey was a matchmaker by trade. And had, God help her, set herself up with the octopus in the three-piece suit back there. Her new compatibility prediction system must suck rotten eggs to have been so very wrong about this guy being suited for her.

"No habla inglés." The cab driver shook his head at her while staring unrepentantly at her breasts.

"You don't need to speak English." She pointed to the address again, a series of numbers and a street name that should be easily recognizable for a guy in his profession.

The bar wasn't exactly in a busy part of town, so walking was out of the question. This was a crappy way to begin her working vacation, a vacation she'd ultimately convinced herself was for her own good. Not just because Laura had said so, but also because Lacey feared her matchmaking site's problems could be traced back to her losing touch with how the dating world worked.

How many dates had she been on since college? She could count them on one hand. And the number of guys she'd dated more than once…exactly two. Neither of them had lasted more than a few months before Lacey had gone back to her work and her isolated island. She'd decided that her Puerto Rico trip needed to be about more than meeting her ninety-six-percent match. She would do some serious dating research down here. Check out the singles world as the locals knew it and blog about it in detail for her Web site to drive up her visitor numbers during this one last push to beat her sister.

She sighed at the driver's comfortable sprawl where he sipped a Coke and listened to Spanish talk radio. The only illumination came from the bar, casting the street in shadow except for the occasional set of headlights cruising in or out of the parking lot.

"Are you okay?" A voice from behind her—and, praise God, an English-speaking voice—distracted her from waving the paper in the cabbie's face again.

Turning, she discovered the man who'd saved her in the bar. A clean-cut, square-jawed type who looked so all-American he could have strolled off a Ralph Lauren ad. The dimple in his chin only added to the impression. Sure, he wore a wife-beater shirt and Bermuda shorts like most of the rest of the guys in the surfer hangout, but something about his earnest expression communicated that he was a stand-up guy.

Assuming she had *any* judgment where men were concerned. A major leap of faith in light of the bozo she'd just walked away from.

"I'm fine." Straightening, she stepped away from the driver to introduce herself. "I'm sorry I didn't take more time to thank you properly back there. I'm Lacey Sutherland."

He glanced from her face to her hand and back again

before he took her fingers and squeezed. Gently. Warmly. Definitely a nice touch.

"Damon Craig. And you're welcome." He pointed up the street. "You want a ride back to your hotel before your admirer gets out here? My car is just up there."

It was a nice offer. A gentlemanly offer. The kind of white-knight suggestion she would have expected from an all-American male with a dimple in his chin that could make him Tom Brady's younger brother.

But something shifted in the air between them as he asked it. Some boy-girl dynamic that made her heart beat a little faster.

"Um—" She knew better than to trust something as unreliable as physical chemistry as an indicator for compatibility. On any given day the Connections message board received a post about a relationship based on lust that went awry. "I'd better not."

From behind Damon, the door of the bar swung open with a squeak and a bang. Three guys piled out onto the steps of Café Rosita, two in silk shirts and dress pants and one in a banker's suit with a pastel-pink tie. Nick Castine.

Before she had time for dismay, Captain All-America spun her around, tucking her close to his side as he wrapped his arm about her waist. With his free hand, he cradled her head to his chest as if to hide her from the world. All at once, he was steering her away from the street, down a sandy path through palm trees, her heels sinking in the soft terrain.

Oddly, she could hardly protest when her cheek rubbed against his chest, her nose picking up the sudden tantalizing scent of man and aftershave. The warmth of his body plastered against hers, making her keenly aware that Damon Craig wasn't just a do-gooder "guy next door" giving her a hand. He was a major, muscle-bound stud.

Who happened to smell good enough to eat.

"What are you doing?" She tripped on a piece of driftwood and realized the ocean must be nearby. She could hear the roll of waves in one ear while the beat of Damon's heart thumped against the other.

"You don't want to run into that touch-happy jackass again." Damon peered back up the hill and steered her to the right along a line of palm trees, relinquishing his hold on her. "We can wait down here until he takes off."

She felt adrift suddenly, her skin cooling in the aftermath of those moments tucked up against him. Even her legs felt a little more unsteady. She dropped her laptop bag to the ground and took in the sights—a fat full moon reflecting white light on frothy waves rolling with a swish to her feet.

"You seemed to handle him just fine back in the bar." Not that she expected him to fight all her battles for her. But he sure hadn't looked intimidated by Nicholas earlier.

"Yeah, and he's probably had just enough time to feel the full sting to his ego, so I wouldn't count on handling him so easily the next time."

"I don't know how I could have ended up with such a loser." She was tempted to crack open her laptop and pore over the data again to see what she might have missed. She hadn't spent months working on the new compatibility software to end up making mistakes like this.

"You're not the first person to misjudge a date." He

picked up a piece of driftwood and whipped it into the ocean, boomerang-style.

"You don't understand. It's my job to craft an intelligent matchmaking profile system for my company and this is the ninety-six-percent-compatibility match I got paired up with." The reality of it still blew her away. This could mean the whole system she'd spent months on was worthless. She didn't mourn the loss of a dating prospect, since she wasn't looking for romance anyhow. But she sure as heck regretted that her system could be so deeply flawed. "I mean it when I say this should *not* have happened."

He went still—silent—for so long that she noticed it in spite of her preoccupation with the glitch in her program.

"What?" She suspected a guy who looked like Damon Craig had never felt the need to try out matchmaking online.

Women probably threw themselves at him on a regular basis.

"You work for one of those online dating places?"

"Why?" She couldn't help a little defensiveness. "Are you a nonbeliever?"

"To each his own." He didn't elaborate, but then, she'd run into most every type of resistance to her line of work.

"You're absolutely right. Some people don't mind venturing off blindly into the dating world, while others of us prefer to up the odds of success." It was a standard defense of her work, although she found it tough to stand behind it tonight when her projected match had been a grabber. He'd seemed nice enough at first, but his manners had disappeared after his second drink.

Slipping out of her heels, Lacey let her bare feet sink

into the sand. The sensation felt amazing, reminding her that the years she'd kept delaying a vacation had added up. What was wrong with her that she couldn't ever give herself a break to soak up some sun? Feel the sand in her toes? Just because she lived on an island of her own didn't mean she had a beach like this that felt like a deluxe spa treatment on her skin. She had stiff, squishy St. Augustine grass and a view she usually only enjoyed from a window. Maybe she'd do a better job on her software revamp this week if she did it with a tequila sunrise in hand.

"Yeah?" Damon stalked closer and her heart did that fast-forward thing again. "I find it hard to believe a woman like you would need the help of some high-tech program to get a date."

Did he think that only a woman wearing tortoiseshell eyeglasses and her hair in a bun needed help with finding an appropriate man? She wanted to feel defensive, except that she caught another hint of his aftershave scent and experienced a sharp pang of inexplicable awareness.

"Who are you?" She couldn't help the question. She told herself it was in the name of research. "I mean—are you a traveler or a local? I don't know anything about you."

She'd wanted to ask what he did for a living since the information was one of the most telling details on a matchmaking profile. Her gut told her he was all wrong for her, but she wanted the data to back that up, if only to reaffirm her instincts. Because aside from her misstep with Nicholas Castine, she still had faith in the compatibility program she'd designed that was based on tried-and-true personality profiling.

"I'm a hell of a lot better than the punk who just tried to grope you in full view of fifty bar patrons, that's for sure." He didn't look anything like the guy next door right now. Not even the dimple in his chin could erase her impression that this man could be dangerous.

The change in his demeanor didn't frighten her. And that was saying something, because she was a woman who'd never felt at ease around men, after one of her stepfathers had tried to touch her inappropriately.

In theory, Damon Craig's chest-thumping declaration ought to put her on guard. In reality, she found it oddly comforting that he could be so incensed on her behalf. She knew the full-body tingle humming over her skin right now had more to do with an unwise attraction than any inkling of impending harm.

"I'm sure you are a much nicer man than Nicholas—"

"But you're not in the market for nice, right?" He sounded vaguely irritated about that and she wondered why.

"I'm in the market for understanding the laws of physical attraction and how we respond to them." Somehow just uttering the phrase "physical attraction" around him made her knees weak.

A warm breeze blew off the ocean and sent her skirt tickling around her thighs. She'd shopped for something pretty and feminine to wear tonight, throwing herself into the idea of her date so much that she'd actually been disappointed on a personal level when Nicholas had turned out to be all wrong for her. But the pent-up romantic hopes—so totally unexpected—had left her feeling restless and edgy. Her gaze lingered on Damon's broad shoulders as he blocked her view of the water, his big, athletic body communicating in its own language to hers.

His teeth flashed white in the moonlight as he hovered over her.

"That's where you're looking at it all wrong. There are no laws when it comes to attraction." He leaned closer, his gaze dropping to her mouth. "It just drop-kicks you when you least expect it."

His stance on the subject made no sense. The sultry heat rolling off him in waves, however, made one hell of a case to a woman who hadn't indulged herself in far too long.

2

DAMON HADN'T MEANT to tangle with the woman from the bar.

From what he'd gathered from seeing her in action, she was uptight, tied to her technology and had piss-poor street smarts, if she blindly agreed to a computer's choice for a date. Lacey Sutherland seemed more concerned with some bogus scientific research than her personal safety, given that she'd made no arrangements for transportation home tonight. Unless, of course, she was lying about everything and was somehow connected to the drug runner in ways she wouldn't admit.

If she was covering up a more illicit tie to Castine, she was doing a damn good job of it. The last woman he'd known with ties to a drug dealer—his former girlfriend—hadn't hidden the signs of her addiction well. Kelly had run off with her supplier while Damon was on duty, claiming she couldn't take Damon's dangerous and unpredictable job anymore.

Damon had vented his anger about the whole thing through his job over the last year, taking a new, special interest in his drug-interdiction flights. They'd been following small leads to the highest guy in the food chain for months, finally discovering Castine's import-export business at the root of a complex network. His unit didn't want to haul him in until they caught him in the act, and that meant being ready for the next big shipment.

Now his unofficial surveillance was a bust, since he'd made himself conspicuous in the bar tonight. He didn't have anything else to do right now besides prove his point about attraction, especially since he wanted to keep tabs on anyone with a connection to Castine.

Lacey sighed and tapped her foot. At first Damon thought she was being impatient with him, but then she looked up at him and shook her head, blond curls flying.

"I don't agree." She didn't back away from him even though he'd come to rest mere inches from her on the beach below Café Rosita's. Above them the sounds of laughter and reggaeton drifted on the breeze.

"You don't?" He'd half forgotten what they'd been talking about and he rewound their conversation in his mind. He'd been too busy weighing the merits of getting close to her to recall how her words fit.

"No. There are some predictable rules of…attraction." She licked her lips, a small, nervous gesture at odds with her matter-of-fact tone. "Any unexpected feelings that—as you say—drop-kick you unexpectedly, you've got to chalk up to lust. Those are superficial feelings that have little to do with a true emotional and mental chemistry."

"That's rich." He would have laughed if he hadn't been wound tight as a drum from the potent combination of her nearness and the distinct sexual draw of her tongue moistening the soft fullness of her lip. "You're telling me that if you meet someone and they make you all hot inside, that's superficial?"

She twitched at the mention of heat, one hand reaching up to run through her cropped blond curls before she fisted her fingers at her side.

"That's right."

He locked gazes with her for a long moment, breathing in the sultry air between them and growing more sure of himself with every rapid rise and fall of her breasts under the skimpy yellow triangles of fabric that made up the top of her dress.

"And if you can't catch your breath because your thoughts have turned to pleasure, that doesn't matter, either?"

The pink tip of her tongue darted out once more.

"I really don't think—"

"What about if your mouth goes dry just thinking about being touched by a stranger?" He closed the last inch of space between them, his thighs bumping hers, their hips grazing.

She inhaled sharply and her breasts pressed against him for one pulse-pounding second.

"None of it matters if there's nothing underneath to hold two people together." She might have moved to back him up, her hand splaying across his chest, glossy pink nails flexing ever so slightly into his skin.

But she didn't push him away, perhaps as intrigued by the feel of him as he was by her.

"And how the hell do you know none of it matters?" He cornered her with words since he wouldn't press her physically. She'd been manhandled already tonight. Damon would be damned if he'd hold a woman who didn't want him. "Have you ever done any of your research on this so-called superficial level of attraction?"

She blinked up at him, her eyes wide with surprise at the very idea. Or maybe she was just shocked to discover that bumping hips and flirting with a total stranger could be one hell of a good time.

In fact, that same set of circumstances might account for why Damon was suddenly fuzzy on the whys and wherefores of what he wanted to prove to her. Because right now, he could only seem to recall that he wanted her, hot and hungry and flexing her pink fingernails against him.

"My research must be a tad…thin in that area. I don't date much to start with. And this latest episode was a particular low point. But I think we all experience that impulse to…get close to someone." She flattened her hand to his chest and rubbed down his abs to his hover above his belt. "I think I've ignored that impulse for too long."

Did she mean it? Or was she leading him on until he was on such a short freaking leash that he would lunge like a rabid dog at the least enticement? If she was an associate of Castine's out to set him up, he needed to be careful. But, damn it, he'd ignored his own sexual impulses for too long, as well. They seemed to be breathing in the same pheromones.

"I don't want to catch you on the rebound." He skimmed his fingers up her arm, feeling the way her skin pebbled as she shivered. "So maybe I'd better let you go."

He was ready to back off. Hell, he needed to back off.

"I normally play it safe," she informed him. "But this week, I'm on vacation from my real life."

He might have responded, but then she wrapped her arms around him and kissed him.

His brain stopped in second gear while the rest of him

responded on instinct. Her lips were incredibly soft, the contact the barest brush of her mouth on his as if she was conducting another scientific test, waiting to see how long it took to prompt him into sensual overdrive. When other women had approached him this year, he'd turned them down flat, his interest in dating seriously compromised after Kelly. But he couldn't find any of that cool indifference now.

He pulled her closer to press her hips to his, chest to chest, belly to belly. If Lacey Sutherland turned out to be a lead, at least she was one that he wouldn't let go.

Kissing her was a supercharge to his senses, bombarding him with desire for her from every angle. She tasted like sweet rum and her tongue tangled with his for dominance. She arched up on her toes, her body stretched delectably over his.

Her hum of pleasure ratcheted up the heat, a mating call he couldn't resist after a year of abstaining from women altogether. He hadn't even been tempted since Kelly, but now his body protested every one of the last 360-some days of restraint.

All at once things turned carnal.

He plunged his hand into her hair, tilting her head to just the right angle. She seemed to melt under his touch, her whole body shifting, heating, accommodating to every adjustment. Blood pulsed through him with new, fiery need, pounding his temples and narrowing his focus to this woman who felt, smelled, tasted so exactly right.

She strained against him as if she couldn't get close enough. He lifted her, needing her tight against him. She moaned as he backed her into a coconut tree for better leverage. He reached down to the hem of her skirt and, lifting one of her legs, he wrapped it around his waist. The move positioned the hot core of her against the throb between his legs.

For a moment the contact felt exquisite. But that wasn't enough to quench what he wanted. And she sure as hell didn't behave like a woman who'd had enough yet. With a squeal, she brought her other leg up and crooked it about his hips, locking her ankles at his waist. Sealing them together.

The sensation was so raw. So dark and primal he didn't even think about fighting it. Hell, right now, he couldn't think why he shouldn't have her. She'd said she was on vacation from real life. Maybe right now so was he.

He pushed up her skirt just enough to reach under with his hands. Her silky thighs quivered at his touch, every inch of her so responsive to him he felt like King-freaking-Midas. Her skin got hotter and hotter as he reached the lace-trimmed leg of her panties.

Hunger ripped through him, her scent making him crazy as he slipped his fingers beneath the lace to touch her. She arched into his hand, pressing herself to him, demanding more.

He traced the slick folds of her feminine flesh, her body already wet and ready for him. Had he done this to her? And she wanted to write it all off as a kind of attraction that didn't matter?

Determined to make her see things differently, he released her lips to kiss the long, sexy column of her throat. The soft sounds she made, urging him on, had him ready to undo his belt right there. She clutched his shoulders and his hips, clinging to him, and he couldn't see past her or the moment to slow down.

Instinctively he knew what to do to draw out her response, her slick heat pulsating with need as he stroked her into a gasping, twitching frenzy. He could feel how swollen she was, knew she was so close and—

A light flashed across the beach behind him, casting a blue-white glow on Lacey's skin for a moment.

"Crap." Damon stepped away from the tree, steadying Lacey in his arms even though her legs remained locked tight around him. Reason returned to him with the force of a pistol whip to the jaw. What the hell was he doing when he hadn't even checked this woman out yet?

"What?" Her fingers teased down the back of his neck as she leaned into him again.

"It's a shore patrol." The worst possible kind of company while he had a woman—quite possibly a drug runner's accomplice—backed up against a tree. "The Coast Guard."

LACEY TRIED to blink through the fog of unprecedented lust to figure out what Damon was talking about. Out in the water, she spotted a boat carrying a mounted searchlight making a slow pass along the shoreline where they stood—at least, where Damon stood, while she clung to him as if she hadn't had a man in years.

She was hanging by a thread, letting her guard down, her inhibitions down and her panties…well, sideways. And he cared what the Coast Guard thought?

"What are they going to do about a little harmless tongue tangling on the beach?" She touched his cheek to encourage his gaze back to her since the man's neck had craned around at a good hundred-plus degrees.

"Shit." Strengthening his hold on her, he took off

running through the coconut trees and undergrowth as the searchlight began to track back toward them.

His hands gripped her thighs through her dress, her weight seeming like no concern to him as he made impressive time back up the hill toward the bar.

"My laptop!" she protested, holding tight to his shoulders as she ducked her head into his neck. "I left everything down there."

She didn't even have her shoes on.

"I'll go back down and get them when the patrol leaves." His words weren't even breathless, as if he carried an extra 120—okay, a fair bit more than that— around with him all the time when he ran.

Which made her wonder...

"Why are we running?" As some common sense started to filter through the lust haze, some of her earlier fears returned. What in the hell was she doing with her legs wrapped around a man she knew nothing about other than that he kissed like a fantasy and hid from military personnel?

"We don't need the hassle of being questioned by a bunch of overzealous seamen tonight."

"But we weren't doing anything wrong." Although there was that pesky issue of public decency. She wriggled her legs loose as he reached the top of the hill at the end of Café Rosita's parking lot.

A couple of cab drivers smoked cigarettes on the curb, but neither one paid them any attention. Other than that, the street was quiet except for the pulsing salsa tune that vibrated the ground beneath them.

"Speak for yourself." He glared out at the searchlight as it traced the beach again.

"Oh my God." She backed up a step toward the cab drivers, preparing to call for help. "You're a drug runner."

His head whipped around and he turned that sexy hot stare of his on her again.

"Hell no." A grin kicked up one corner of his mouth. "I've got to work with those guys. I'll never hear the end of it if their searchlight catches me with a woman."

It took a few seconds for the information to sink into a brain that had already switched into panic mode.

"You're Coast Guard?" She sized up his short hair, that suited a military man just fine, and his Bermuda shorts and wife-beater shirt that didn't.

"Lieutenant Damon Craig, at your service." He flashed a military ID under her nose before he grabbed her hand and tugged her back into the relative shelter of coconut trees. "Sorry to give you a scare. A shore patrol would never bust up a couple kissing on the beach, but if they knew it was me—" He shrugged as he gave her a self-deprecating grin. "The guys can be brutal to each other."

Relief flooded her veins that he wasn't a bad guy, the adrenaline letdown all the more powerful after being so keyed up for him just minutes ago.

"You're a military man." She finally had the answer to her question about what he did for a living.

Shuffling this new bit of information around in her head, she was already pulling together his dating profile. Coast Guard lieutenant and incredible kisser seeks…what? A hot time on the beach with a total stranger? Would he expect a follow-up performance after that kiss? She'd been upset after the way Nicholas treated her, and she'd let that fuel some of her need to get close to Damon.

And oh my, she needed to get out more. She could hardly control herself with the first man she'd kissed in ages.

"There's an air station at Borinquen, not far from here." He gestured vaguely with a jerk of his thumb. "Let me go get your laptop and shoes. I'll give you a ride back to your hotel."

And because she was tongue-tied and completely out of her element about how to behave with a stranger she'd just let fondle her intimately on a public beach, Lacey nodded mutely.

In no time, he returned with everything she'd left behind, reminders of her purpose here in Puerto Rico. Because even though the date with Nicholas hadn't worked out, that didn't mean she'd just sit idle until she lost the competition with Laura. She needed to post exciting new content on her site if she wanted to beat Laura's visitor numbers. Since she wouldn't blog about her failed date, she'd have to rely on her Plan B material. She'd get out to explore the singles scene here and blog about it. She'd check and recheck the new compatibility system and hope she could implement it before the month-long competition was over.

"It's this way." He pointed the way to his car as he handed over her shoes.

Warily, she brushed as much sand off as she could before strapping on the teal-colored high-heeled sandals that had made her feel so glamorous earlier. Now she felt oddly vulnerable as the night had gotten completely out of hand.

"I can't." She straightened, refusing to follow him. "I think I'd better call it a night, Damon."

He turned, paused and sauntered back toward her. His slow pace made a new tension tighten in her belly. Sure, she still felt the tingle of red-hot awareness that had been kick-started into overdrive on the beach. But now that feeling mingled with wariness because she knew the formidable sway he held over her. She'd never met a man who could raze her barriers the way he had in mere minutes.

For that matter, no man had ever *dented* her barriers, period. She was an expert about holding back. Ensuring no one ever had enough of her to hurt her.

"I've offended you." He seemed to offer his own explanation for why she refused to ride home with him.

"Of course not." She reached for her laptop and tugged it gently from his grip. "I just…feel awkward. I'd be more comfortable taking a cab if you would be kind enough to explain to one of those drivers that I need to get to the Hotel Aquadilla."

Nodding, he finally relinquished her bag and she put it over her shoulder. Having her computer and her phone close by made her feel slightly more in control.

As long as they didn't kiss again. This man could destroy her willpower with one heavy-lidded look. And, sweet heaven, she couldn't believe how quickly she'd lost control back on that beach.

"Not a problem. But can you tell me one thing?"

"Ask away." She didn't know whether to be relieved or disappointed that he'd given up on driving her back to the hotel so easily. A ridiculous, contrary notion of course. But her body still throbbed with the unmet need he'd stirred deep inside her. Had he shut off that switch so quickly? Or was he simply better at hiding sexual frustration? She couldn't imagine how she'd ever fall asleep while images of what might have happened plagued her overheated imagination.

She'd never, ever taken a sexual encounter so far, so fast. She usually had big-time issues with physical intimacy considering her past. Yet with Damon, she'd felt normal. Desirable. And so hot she thought she'd never cool down again.

"Are you still convinced there are rules for attraction?" He reached up to caress her bottom lip ever so softly with his thumb.

The touch distracted her at first, calling to her every overwrought nerve ending and making her lose sight of the question. The effect this man had on her was so far out of her realm of experience that she didn't know what to do with it. But then, as her eyes drifted half-closed, her brain caught up with her body and she processed the words.

Her eyes flew open.

"Absolutely. I've staked a career on it." Defensiveness crept back, replacing all those feel-good endorphins. Was he challenging her work again?

His hand fell away.

"I thought maybe the kiss convinced you that compatibility isn't always predictable." His jaw clenched, the action highlighting the dimple in his chin. "I'm curious about the kind of work you do. I've never met a matchmaker before."

"And I've never met a Coast Guard lieutenant who gave me such a hard time about it before." She smiled to take the bite out of her words. She wasn't used to pickup lines, and she thought Damon might be angling to see her again.

Something she really shouldn't allow, as much as her body hummed with pleasure at the very thought. Now that her date with Nicholas had fallen through, she needed to bolster the blog with exciting new content, since she had no personal online dating experience to chronicle, the way she'd hoped when she'd come down here.

"I wonder why you're so convinced you can predict who's going to be attracted to whom." He stared at her, contemplative.

"I can't. I can only predict compatibility, and attraction doesn't equal compatibility." A fact she was quickly recalling the longer she tried to carry on a conversation with him. He was still essentially a stranger even though she'd just let him touch her in ways that made her blush to think about. They didn't have anything in common besides a case of red-hot lust, apparently. "Thank you for helping me out earlier. Now I'd better find a ride home."

Brushing past him, she marched toward the cabbies, who seemed to have finished their smoking break and now watched the disagreement unfolding.

Digging in her laptop case, she removed the address for her hotel again and tossed it toward one of the drivers, determined to make herself understood.

"Hotel Aquadilla, *por favor.*" And, without waiting for him to agree, she marched straight to the back door of the taxi and slid into the seat.

"I'm just saying it can be good to follow your instincts now and then," Damon called to her from somewhere back in the parking lot, his voice growing closer as if he'd started the trek to his own car.

"Good night, Damon," she called out the window,

catching a glimpse of his square shoulders headed up the street.

Ignoring the tug of regret in her belly, she recalled one of the reasons she'd come to Puerto Rico was to prove to her sister she could have, in Laura's words, a good time. Aw, hell. Funny to think the man she'd just kissed like there was no tomorrow had also encouraged her to act on instinct.

In light of how exciting their kiss had been, she would say she'd already checked the box on thrills for this vacation. Now she needed to get back to work and figure out why she'd been set up with a dud like Castine.

While that plan made good logical sense, Lacey knew that playing it safe would also mean she'd probably never see Damon Craig again. What if that meant she'd never experience another kiss like the one they'd just shared?

All at once, she had new appreciation for the visitors to her Web site who resisted their smart, compatible matches for the sake of sexual chemistry with someone who was all wrong for them. If nothing else, her night with Damon had made sure she knew exactly how tough it was to walk away from the most delectable of temptations.

3

"YOU'VE GOTTA FIND this girl." Enrique huffed out the words as he pumped iron, his forearm curling a dumbbell twice the size of his head. Veins popped out along his wrist as he worked out next to Damon.

They sat in the base gym on nearby weight benches, the clank of iron muted by the heavy-metal music blaring over a crappy stereo system.

"You think she's connected to the drug ring?" Damon had wrestled with that possibility all night long.

He hadn't told Enrique all the dirty details of the night before, but they typically hit the gym at the same time on the weekends and the lieutenant-JG had pushed him for highlights of what had happened after Damon left the bar with Lacey.

It was a topic he hadn't been eager to revisit. He'd been working damn hard to put her out of his head after he'd done a preliminary background search this morning, and she came up clean.

Hard being the operative word. He'd swum laps in his condo's pool at 3:00 a.m. in an attempt to cool his jets, but sleep had eluded him until just before sunrise. At which point he'd dreamed about her, his brain supplying an endless variety of scenarios in which they'd finished what they'd started last night.

"What's wrong with you, man?" Enrique rested his weight for a ten-count before he started his next set of reps. "If I let some innocent chick wander around town, oblivious to the fact that she'd pissed off a drug pusher and possible sexual predator with an ego as big as Texas, I'd like to think you'd tell me to get my head out of my ass." He paused in his reps. "Sir."

Damon shook his head, not giving a rip about protocol. Crewing together on an HH65-A "Dolphin" helicopter, they'd been stationed together twice before Borinquen, Damon as a pilot while Enrique served as a rescue swimmer. Their shared time on duty included a three-year stint in Alaska where they'd saved each other's butts from killer waves, frostbite, broken ice floes, a couple of pirates and one pissed-off polar bear. When no one else was around, Uncle Sam's rankings didn't really come into play.

"You think he'd go after someone like her? Someone the whole bar saw him with?" The memory of Nick Castine's hands on Lacey made his gut burn with surprising heat.

No matter that Damon had done some groping of his own. He hadn't moved on her against her will.

"You know how these guys are. They build their gangs on an alpha-dog pecking order. Castine sees himself as top of the pack and he wants to make damn sure everyone around him recognizes his dominance. Besides, the jury's still out on whether he's a run-of-the-mill sex addict or more of a full-out predator. He could have targeted this girl for more attention either way."

Damon bit off a ripe curse. He knew Castine's file as well as Enrique did. Knew about the sidebar on his personal behavior. But since his sexual tendencies hadn't affected how he dealt drugs so far, the information had remained in the background of the investigation.

Settling a weight bar back into its cradle, he knew Enrique was right. Even if there was a small chance he was right, Damon owed it to Lacey to warn her about Castine.

"How am I going to alert her without compromising our investigation?" He'd been pushing his luck to confront the guy in Rosita's last night. But then, drug runners and Coasties had been sharing the same port watering holes since the USCG was born, so Damon had told himself it wouldn't necessarily tip off Castine to the military's interest in him.

"Tell her it's a matter of national security. Encourage her to board a plane and get the hell out of town. Or, at the very least, see if she'd consider staying in San Juan while she's down here."

That made sense, although after the way Damon had needled her about her career last night, he suspected he wouldn't have much luck convincing her of anything.

"We didn't part on the best terms." Major understatement.

"Big surprise there." Enrique changed arms with the barbell, his gaze fixed on a petty officer who'd transferred in the week before. The woman claimed a spot on a pull-up bar and proceeded to raise herself in lightning-quick reps.

"What the hell does that mean?"

Damon was edgy after no sleep, but it seemed like Enrique was doing his level best to needle him.

"You've lost all charm with the ladies since Kelly left you." Rolling the barbell aside, Enrique started toward the pull-up bar and then turned back. "But even though you push the chicks away, you gotta ask yourself why you went over to rescue little Miss Muffett last night when I was right there and could have done the deed."

He shrugged, directing his attention back toward the petty officer as he strode to the other side of the gym.

"That's because your idea of saving the day is buying a round of drinks for everyone," Damon called, gathering up his towel as he headed for the showers. "I didn't think the situation called for peacemaking, savvy?"

But Enrique was already engrossed in conversation with the pull-up queen. Which meant Damon would have to finalize a plan to see Lacey on his own.

"Lost all my charm, my ass," he muttered as he shoved his way into the locker room, sweat rolling down his forehead and his chest. "She'll probably be thrilled to see me."

THE LAST PERSON Lacey expected to approach her at her hotel's poolside bar the next day was Nicholas Castine.

She peered up at him through her pink-rimmed sunglasses, an umbrella drink in one hand as she scrolled through the Connections Web site blog on her laptop with the other.

"Sorry to surprise you, Lacey," he repeated, smoothing a hand down his silk tie—lavender today. "I won't stay and certainly don't want to bother you, but I wanted to apologize in person for my behavior last night."

"How thoughtful." She managed a tight smile before returning to the work on her laptop. "I'll admit I had higher expectations for our date."

She didn't plan to let him off the hook easily, still

annoyed that her matchmaking profiling system had steered her toward someone who'd treated her the way he had. But then again, because the system had chosen him as one of her top three matches, she was marginally curious to hear what he had to say in his defense. They'd exchanged several pleasant e-mails before arranging to meet. He'd even supplied a lot of great information about the singles' scene in Puerto Rico for her dating research.

"I realize that. And I guess I had the wrong impression about your expectations since you traveled so far for our date." He accepted a drink from a waitress wearing khaki shorts and a polo shirt with the hotel name on it. He dropped a sizable bill on her tray but wisely did not try taking a seat on the deck lounger next to Lacey. "I overstepped last night because most women I meet these days—they expect to move quickly."

She said nothing, unsure how to respond until he clarified that remark. Was he suggesting she'd dressed too provocatively for their date? Or that women in general wanted to jump into bed with him shortly after meeting him? Of course, she had little room to judge him when she'd been quick to speed things along physically with another man last night….

The memory of Damon Craig's touch was enough to torch her concentration into smoldering ash. Her eyes lingered on the same line of data on her computer screen, unable to go forward when scintillating snippets from the night before distracted her.

"That's no excuse, I know," Nick went on, tipping a short glass of a dark amber liquid to his lips. "But honestly, most women I've met online have been looking for hook-ups more than, ah, time to get to know each other."

He set the glass on a small table between them where she'd rested her cell phone and her purse, looking ready to leave. And she was more than happy to see him go since she had zero tolerance for manhandling losers.

But that was in her personal life. In her professional life, she could at least afford to set aside her distaste for the man long enough to give him the third-degree on what he'd entered in his matchmaking profile.

"Wait." The man represented the most significant dating research she'd done down here, and if she wanted to launch a public version of her new dating-software service when she returned this month—and keep her sister from wiping her off the Web during this contest— she needed to know about any bugs in the system.

"Yes?" He still kept that polite distance, the excess of personal space assuring her he wouldn't touch her.

"Have you been using Connections exclusively?"

She hated the idea that her company's matchmaking site had been invaded by singles who wanted to transplant the bar scene experience to their online dating. At that rate, she wasn't doing any more than pimping people out for sex.

Eeeww.

"Shh." He lifted a finger to his lips, smiling through the shushing as he sat down on a lounger nearby. "Using a matchmaking service is nothing I advertise. But I travel so much that it has become more difficult to meet women. And yes, I've only worked with Connections."

She wanted to ask him how he'd tricked her system into thinking he was so great when he was a touch-happy groper, and then decided maybe she didn't have enough professional determination for this little interview after all. She wanted him gone.

But then he leaned closer and lowered his voice.

"You know, since you and I didn't work out, I'm trying something new to meet people at the end of the week. It's like a ship-wide speed-dating event on a party barge that leaves out of Rincon Friday night." He pulled a pair of shades out of his jacket pocket and slid them onto his nose. "If you want, I can look up the details and leave them at the front desk if you're interested."

"No, thanks." She kept her tone clipped. And she folded her laptop to end the conversation.

"Lacey." A second man's voice startled her, the tone instantly recognizable from over her shoulder. "May I have a word with you? Alone?"

Damon Craig strode into view, his six-foot frame clad in a pair of cargo pants and a T-shirt. He wore a long-sleeve blue dress shirt unbuttoned and rippling in the breeze. He cast a hard stare at Nicholas, a silent testosterone war flaring up between them.

"Of course," she replied easily, determined to douse the he-man strutting before it got out of control. "Nick, thanks for stopping by."

To her relief, the other man nodded, his eyes fixing on her instead of Damon Craig, who'd just strode into their conversation uninvited.

Did he think she was going to melt in his arms again like the night before? Indignation stiffened her spine at the memory of how easily she'd let herself be carried away.

"Once again, you have my apologies. I'll drop off

that information to you later in the week in case you change your mind." Without a word to Damon, the American businessman departed, attracting admiring glances from every woman within fifty feet of him.

Women who didn't know about his air of entitlement or his assumption that every female around wanted to sleep with him.

Still, her outrage at Castine's nerve didn't compare to her surprise at seeing Damon again. The indefinable appeal of the Coast Guard lieutenant had not diminished overnight, had not suffered for their abrupt goodbye. Her whole body hummed with vital awareness of his even though he stood some ten feet distant.

"What information?" He swung on her without prelude, stalking closer. "I can't believe you're even talking to that guy after how he treated you last night."

Lowering himself into the deck lounger beside her, Damon's long legs sprawled against the wooden slats of her chair.

"Hello to you, too." Her gaze darted to his hands and she experienced a vivid flashback to those long fingers gliding up her thigh. The memory was so good it hurt, especially since it hadn't culminated in the ultimate payoff.

"Lacey, I mean it." He leaned forward, his big, buffed shoulders blocking out anything and everything but him from her line of sight. "What did that guy want with you?"

Remembering now exactly what she hadn't liked about *this guy* she took a deep breath and prepared to tell him where to get off.

"*He* came to apologize, which is more than I can say

for you." Swiveling away from him, she slid her feet
back into her high-heeled espadrille sandals and retrieved her laptop.

"Wait." Damon's command fell on deaf ears. But
then he touched her and all bets were off.

It was just a gentle brush of his fingers along her
shoulder, a skim of hot male warmth against the thin
gauze tunic she wore to cover her bathing suit. But it
damn near short-circuited her brain.

"I really need to talk to you in private." His deep,
masculine voice sent a shiver over her skin, the sound
pooling pleasantly at the base of her spine. "Please."

By the time he deployed the operative word of good
manners she was toast anyhow.

"I can't be alone with you." She risked a glance over
her shoulder and found his face too close to hers, too
much in kissing range.

"We can go to your room." He stood, drawing her to
her feet with a hand under her elbow before he released
her again. "I'll even promise to keep my hands to
myself, okay?"

She halted there, uncertain of herself, of him, of what
the hell she was thinking to let him join her in a hotel
suite surrounded by a tropical paradise. But he was
already taking her laptop case and waiting for her to
head back inside.

For three measured heartbeats she stalled. Hoped
she hadn't taken leave of her senses. Damon Craig had
no place in this vacation—dating him wouldn't be the
blog publicity stunt she'd hoped would drive more
traffic to Connections and the new online dating program she'd developed.

"Lacey?" He turned to check on her progress, impatience evident in the tense line of his shoulders.

She wasn't frightened of him in the least, so she could hardly use that as an excuse to avoid him. If anything, she was simply afraid of her response to him, more powerful than any chemistry she'd ever had with a man. Still, if she could pinpoint what drew her to him…

She would increase her level of empathy with her Web site clients, that was for damn sure. Maybe her whole career would improve if she came off her island a little more often to remember what dating was like. She could only push her matchmaking expertise for so long as a single woman before clients would wonder why she couldn't find a good match for herself.

Was she totally justifying her desire to spend more time with the übersexy Coast Guard lieutenant? Probably. But how could she resist the only man she'd ever met who made her feel sensual, desirable and not in the least afraid to test her wings in the sex department? After growing up insecure and overweight, it had taken years to feel good about herself.

Damon advanced on her, his expression closed, the set to his jaw broadcasting frustration.

"I'm coming," she assured him, hurrying his way. Her new plan filled her with excitement, a bubble of sexual eagerness floating along her skin with a barely there caress. She let her eyes wander over Damon and then lowered her voice. "Or at least I will be soon."

SEX WAS ON HIS MIND again.

Nick Castine lingered in the shadows of the hotel lobby, watching another predator scoop up the tasty little morsel he'd left behind. Lacey Sutherland had been a coup for him—a testament to the sheer genius of his new method of finding women to feed sexual needs that had blown out of control in the past six months.

Watching her now, Nick allowed the frustration to burn inside him. It had been simple enough to slide his profile into the Connections matchmaking program. Their security was outdated. His picture—under three revolving aliases—would now show up as a potential match for twenty-five percent of women who used the site. His profile was variable, skewing to mirror the woman's.

But he'd messed up on his date with Lacey. He'd recognized early on that she was a more traditional female, using Connections to meet men interested in long-term relationships. But he'd been high on life last night, psyched about his quick success rigging the dating-service site and flush with money from a recent lucrative deal. He'd moved too fast, allowing the beast inside him too much rein when she would have come willingly enough if he'd given her more time.

Or a potent cocktail laced with the drugs that made his addictions so damn much fun.

Now she was sidled up to the clean-cut dude who had to be a cop or a military man. And she looked all too freaking happy about it. Nick definitely wouldn't tap that ass now without some medicinal aids. Or brute force.

Both of which appealed to him, especially since the bitch had the nerve to call him a lowlife in public. He used to be able to control his urges better. But his addiction had grown so strong that he would have women any way he could get them. He thought about sex constantly, his only relief coming in the few days or sometimes the few hours after an encounter with someone new.

Arranging big-money deals didn't even distract him anymore unless he knew he would be using some of the drugs for recreational use. For paralyzing some tender young female into doing whatever he said and serving his sexual demands for as long as he wished.

No doubt that's how he'd convince Lacey Sutherland to spread her long, luscious legs for him. Her conscious mind might prefer G.I. Joe, but with a few chemical additives, Nick would teach her.

Walking out of the lobby toward the parking lot, he began planning their next encounter. After the way she'd rejected him, he needed to have Lacey in order to clear his mind of her. With the biggest shipment of his career to orchestrate this week, Nick couldn't afford any mental distractions.

That meant the sooner he found a way to bang the blonde, the better.

SMILING WOMEN made him twitchy.

In Damon's experience, that meant they were up to something, hiding something. Of course, a woman like Lacey invited suspicion anyhow. She was traveling alone and meeting in secluded corners of the island with a suspected drug runner. Plus Damon was wildly attracted to her, which made him wary as hell.

The last time he'd gotten hot and bothered about a woman, she'd followed him to the Aleutian Islands, then had fallen in love with some criminal, following him to Tucson while Damon hauled fishermen out of the

Atlantic. She'd called the moving company while he was in the E.R. for hypothermia, in fact.

So yeah, Lacey's cat-who-swallowed-the-canary expression had him flipping out a little bit. He really should just tell her what he needed to and leave. But if Castine was already showing up at her hotel, he had to help her protect herself.

"My room's right here." She gestured to the left where the ocean-view accommodations must be. Real estate wasn't cheap in Puerto Rico, but he knew the waterfront space wasn't bank-breaking, either.

Damon watched her as she withdrew her room key, his skin heating up at the simple, intimate act of a woman letting a man into her hotel room. An act of trust he promised himself he would be worthy of.

He intended to take that "no touching" thing seriously.

"Sorry to call you away from the pool." He held the door wide for her as she walked in first, tossing her keys on a TV stand at the foot of a king-size bed.

The room wasn't palatial, but it was big. Simple white cotton covered the bed in a crisp spread, the numerous pillows all white. A bud vase held a few branches from native plants. The brilliant greens, yellows and oranges seemed all the brighter for the white stucco walls and lack of other decor. But that was Puerto Rico. You could plant toothpicks and harvest plants like these in a year's time. It was a far cry from Air Station Kodiak where a handful of scrappy pine trees were all that could weather the winters.

"It's okay." She dumped her purse in a nearby leather chair and stepped out of her heels, her toenails painted bright fuchsia today. "I probably got enough sun anyhow."

She arched up on her toes for a long, catlike stretch, her back bowing slightly as she yawned and reached a hand up toward the ceiling. The lush display of feminine curves made his mouth go dry, her gauzy cover-up falling open to reveal amazing breasts.

They were high and perfectly proportioned. A delicious mouthful.

"So what did you want to talk to me about…" She still had that mysterious smile on her face and he wondered if she'd caught him ogling her. Not that she looked terribly upset about it. "…in private?"

She twirled one end of the golden braid that served as a belt for her white cover-up. Looking up at him through her inky lashes, he knew damn well she was flirting with him but he didn't know why. She'd been the one to pull away last night, getting all prickly when she thought he'd dismiss her work.

"It's about Nick Castine." He barreled ahead with the mission at hand, unwilling to sit idle in a boat taking on water. He'd tell her what he came here for and that would alter her mood in a hurry. "I have reason to believe he's involved in illegal activities."

Her head came up then. No more coy looks. Nick's shady connections were no big secret to anyone from around here. If she was on the take, he'd just alerted her to their investigation. But if she was a naive tourist to the island, then he was saving her from a hell too horrible to contemplate. He couldn't risk letting her fall into that if there was the least chance she was innocent.

"Other than the occasional ill-advised bar grope?"

A breeze filtered through the open French doors, lifting the hem of her cover-up a fraction of a degree and stirring some kind of tropical scent. Whether it was flowers or perfume, he couldn't say. He could say her thighs would tempt a saint.

"Well beyond." He forced his gaze back to hers. "I can't go into detail since I'm privy to sensitive military intelligence and we have a good inside track on local bad guys. But I thought you should know in case you were able to rearrange your travel plans. I'd advise switching hotels."

Her jaw dropped for a moment, and he could tell he'd frightened her—a condition he simultaneously regretted and celebrated. The sooner she got out of Aquadilla, the better.

"Are we talking violent crime?" Her hand came up to her neck, her fingers gently tugging at the deep vee of her cover-up.

"It's my personal experience that violent crime runs hand in hand with the kinds of offenses he may be committing."

Nodding, she released the neckline of the filmy garment she wore.

"Thank you for the warning. I'll definitely make a hotel transfer. I need to do some research back in San Juan anyhow." She bit her lip, her eyes alighting on the laptop near her bed.

"Would you like some help packing?" He looked around the neat hotel room, thinking he could have her transplanted safely to the city before nightfall. He'd be back on base in no time, his Good Samaritan duties fulfilled. His instincts told him she was honest, no matter that her connection to Castine was incriminating. And following his gut had saved his ass plenty of times before, so he tended to trust those instincts now.

"Are you always this controlling?" She tilted her head to one side, as if she couldn't quite figure him out.

"I don't call it controlling to look out for someone else's safety."

"And I appreciate your coming here to tell me about Nicholas. But now you want to help pack. Yesterday you wanted to do my job for me and prove that no laws govern attraction." She stepped closer to him. Crowding him. "I'd say that's a man who needs to be in charge all the time."

He didn't move a muscle as she walked her hands up his chest, then smoothed them along his shoulders. Her silky touch distracted him when he should be getting her out of here. He had a mission to lead. A unit waiting for him to fly the next segment of surveillance over the Pacific in search of whatever watercraft Castine was using to transport his cargo this time.

"Some people are predisposed to taking charge." He looked down at her plump red lips and wondered how much harm it would do to kiss her again. Was she hell-bent on compatibility? Or would she settle for hot sex? Then again, he was feeling damn compatible with her right about now.

"Some people are also predisposed to arrogance." Shifting her hips, she brushed against his. "And thinking they know what's best for everyone else." She insinuated one slender thigh between his legs.

His pulse spiked. And no matter what mission was waiting for him back on base, this mission with her had moved into code-red terrain.

"I bet I know what's best for you right now." He quit holding back, knowing he wasn't going to get out of this room without addressing the heat between them. "Too bad I promised not to touch you, or else I'd be giving you exactly that."

"You see?" She lifted an eyebrow, all feminine wile and sexual challenge. "You're so convinced you know what I need when you don't know at all."

She reached down and tugged the belt of her cover-up out of the loops. Then, dangling the gold braided leather in front of him, she let the weight swing like a pendulum.

"You want something kinky?" he asked. He couldn't imagine what she hoped to accomplish by presenting him with a leather belt, but he didn't think he could play S & M games, even for a woman who turned him on as much as Lacey did.

Then again…

"Of course not." She lowered the belt and lightly rubbed it across his wrist. "I want to show you that you don't need to be in charge all the time."

His brain took a minute to catch up with his body since he was already envisioning the things he could do to her with the skinny strap. When he finally processed the comment, he couldn't resist a laugh.

"You think *that's* gonna hold me back?" Need for her fired through him, fierce, hot and fast. "I've got news for you, sweetheart. The only thing holding me back from you right now is a promise, and my word has a hell of a lot more power over me than any bond you could ever come up with to hold me down."

Her lips pulled into a soft frown, a lush pout that tempted him to taste her.

"It's up to you, Lacey. I can keep my word and

leave. Or you can release me from it and I'll make you too delirious with pleasure to care that I am very much in charge here."

4

"THOSE ARE some high expectations to live up to." Lacey's knees had, in fact, turned to Jell-O somewhere in the middle of his taunt as they stood in her hotel room.

Delirious with pleasure?

Sign her on. She'd been totally out of her element when she'd implied she might tie him to the bed, but something about Damon Craig made her at ease. She didn't just feel excited. She felt safe with him. The man oozed "protector" from every pore. And, yeah, maybe knowing that made her indulge a side of herself she'd been stifling for years.

"Does that mean yes?" His pulse picked up visibly along the thick column of his neck and she wondered what it would feel like to place her lips over that very spot.

"That means you'd better come with a money-back guarantee if you don't deliver." Her whole body hummed in anticipation, a warm buzz playing along her skin as she waited for his touch.

He still didn't move. His chest raised and lowered with the force of deep breaths, but other than that, he waited as if he had all the time in the world.

"Lacey." His brown eyes narrowed. "Answer the question."

The tension was almost unbearable. The waiting. The wanting. The knowledge that he would deliver. God, she didn't doubt it for a second, even though she liked teasing him.

She opened her lips and found her mouth too dry to speak.

Licking her lips and tasting cherry gloss, she tried again. "Yes. Touch me."

She expected to be overpowered. Backed into the bed. Stripped in a matter of moments. None of which she would have minded. But he didn't do any of those things.

Instead, he tunneled under her open cover-up and wrapped his arms around her. He lifted her up with muscled ease, sliding her body against his so she got the full impact of how much he wanted her. Only when he had her at eye level, her feet dangling an inch or two above the floor, did he kiss her.

His mouth brushed hers gently at first, his lips soft and warm as he pushed hers apart. Normally she was so wary with men. Normally it took them three dates to score even a kiss. But there was something about Damon that overrode her caution and tapped into a fearsome desire she'd never experienced.

He slipped his tongue inside, lavishing hers with long, aching strokes that awakened her every nerve ending. Her fingers gripped his shirt, tangling in the fabric as she fought to withstand the onslaught of intense physical need. His tongue dueled with hers for supremacy until her belly knotted with tension and the sensations made her ache between her thighs.

Arching against him, she urged him closer, already envisioning what that stroke of his tongue would feel like on her breasts. Beneath her bikini bottom. She squirmed at the thought, ready for more. She'd had all the build-up she could take last evening on the beach. Between that round of foreplay and the sex they'd had in her dreams all night, she was primed for him in no time.

"Damon." She pulled his shirt up his back, hitching it on her fingernails and dragging it higher. "Please."

He obliged her by gripping her thighs and wrapping her legs around his waist in a delicious reprise of the night before. Maybe he'd been thinking about what they'd done on the beach as much as she had.

The bulge in his trousers pressed hard against her, and she thought she'd go crazy if she didn't get him more naked soon. With a sweep of her hand, she pulled his shirt the rest of the way off, letting the blue silk float to the floor. She never quit kissing him, but she didn't have to see him to know she'd just un-covered a primo bod. The way he held her effort-lessly proved his strength, honed through military training. And the way the plank of his abs met the ripped muscle of his pecs told her hands all she wanted to know.

"I dreamed about this," he told her, breaking the kiss to stare at her with eyes turned so dark they were almost black. "All night."

"Lucky you, at least you got some sleep." She bent to kiss the indentation centered on his square chin. "I was too keyed up to close my eyes."

She wondered if she should be more guarded with him, but she didn't know how. Her emotions were too stirred up, her senses too overloaded for her to practice her usual restraint.

She reached for his belt, but he cupped her jaw, halting her as he tipped her chin up to look at him.

"It's been a long time for me." His voice had turned gravel harsh, the sound of a man holding himself back. "This first time might get a little out of control."

His eyes glittered with the promise of wicked delights. Intense satisfaction.

"Not as long as it's been for me." Sex had been scarcely more plentiful than her vacations. "I'm more than ready, I promise."

She unfastened his belt as she spoke, freeing the buckle and tugging the leather loose until she found the button for his pants.

She never had the chance to undo it.

He spun her around and strode toward the bed, his long legs making quick work of the bedroom floor. Swinging her down to the white coverlet on the mattress, Damon stood over her. She released his hips, her gaze fastened on his bronzed chest in the muted sunlight filtering through the sheer curtains.

He was an incredible-looking man. Imposing in his masculinity. Fierce in his aspect. No angel's touch of a dimple could detract from the molten fire in his gaze as he unzipped.

Some last strain of cool reason in her head made her reach for the nightstand drawer and pull out the box of condoms she'd bought at the airport. A little vacation wishful thinking.

Stretching out over her, he reached for the box and took the package from her. Every cell inside her responded, his flesh singeing her wherever their bodies met. Their eyes locked for a two-count, whiskey-amber and sea-blue.

The box fell on the bed somewhere beside her ear, but he didn't open it yet. She couldn't process any more than that since his mouth landed on her neck, the wet stroke of his tongue up her throat sending her halfway to orgasm without even trying.

A shudder racked her, tension tightening inside while Damon's chest brushed hers. Hard muscle pressed soft curves, her breasts aching for more. She shifted wordlessly beneath him, arching her back to increase the friction between them. His low growl acknowledged her but he didn't hurry the slow slide of his tongue south. Impatient, she reached behind her neck to untie the top of her bikini.

Damon felt the straps to Lacey's bathing suit loosen and knew he'd run out of time. The woman played with fire so relentlessly he had no choice but to follow the glide of nylon down her skin.

She tasted like sunscreen and coconut, her skin glistening with oil and a new tan. Tan lines. The paler skin around her breasts stood out in the dim room, highlighting the taut pink nipples standing at attention.

Heat flooded him, firing his hands with the need to get her naked. The need to be inside her. Capturing one nipple between his teeth, he rolled the crest along his tongue, drawing hard on her. She whimpered her approval, winding her arms around his neck while he yanked off the rest of her bathing suit top.

The fabric disappeared with satisfying swiftness, leaving her clad in a cover-up that didn't cover much of anything and a bathing suit bottom tied in little bows at her hips. He made quick work of the ties, freeing her from the rest of the dark nylon suit.

Allowing a scant minute to admire the view, he inhaled the fragrance of her. She reached for him, her hands parting the fabric of his boxers before he could get his clothes all the way off.

Didn't matter. Right now, all he cared about was burying himself inside this woman. Her fingers glided over the tip of him, driving him insane with silky strokes where his flesh burned hot.

He kissed her as he returned to the condom box, needing that connection with her while he delayed the deeper union he craved. She was sweet and responsive as he fumbled with the foil packet. He tore the package with one hand before reaching up to free the protection with the other.

"Let me," she whispered, scraping away the silky blond curls from her face as she plucked at the condom.

He held it fast.

"I'm in charge, remember? And twenty hours of foreplay is too long." He worked the condom on with one hand and cupped her mound with the other.

"Then hurry," she urged, tilting her hips into his. "I need—"

He found the swollen flesh between her legs and stroked, cutting off her plea. She held herself very still as he circled the tight nub at her core. Her breath rasped in his ear, the soft puffs of air heating his cheek.

"I know what you need," he assured her, feeling the coiled tension inside her. She was so close to the edge, her face frozen in a mask of rapt anticipation. Pleasure.

He'd never met a woman so easy to read. So responsive that every touch felt combustible. Hell, he'd been hovering on the brink of release for hours himself.

"Damon." She called his name, her eyebrows furrowed. Concentrating. "Damon, please...."

The rush of her orgasm shook her, rocking her whole body in a paroxysm of movement. She arched back, taut as a bow.

A high, keening cry filled the room, the sound of her pleasure piercing his chest and rolling right through him. He didn't wait another second, plunging into her while the aftershocks rocked her. The lush contractions squeezed him, making him grit his teeth against the lure of her body.

Her fingers flexed around his shoulders, her nails raking his skin in a welcome counterpoint to the tight grip of her feminine muscles all around him. He drove his hips deeper, seating himself all the way inside her before withdrawing just enough to start all over again. The rhythm felt elemental, necessary, as if he'd been waiting for this moment from the second he'd laid eyes on her.

She wrapped her legs around him, her smooth thighs pinning his hips tight. He rolled to his side, giving her more room to maneuver without relinquishing a single inch of the connection binding them together. Her cries had turned to soft moans interspersed with incoherent pleas, a litany of sexy murmurs that made him crazy.

Sweat beaded along his forehead, and his back burned with the effort to forestall the inevitable. He wanted to reach between them and stroke another orgasm from her before he came, but his time was running out fast. Between her nails in his shoulders, her thighs vise-locking him and her throaty demands for more, Damon couldn't hold back another second.

Heat rushed through him with a primal surge of possessiveness, a wave of release that tossed him around more thoroughly than any rogue ship in rough waters. He wrapped Lacey close, squeezing her to his chest as the force of his completion shuddered through him.

He might damn well have lost consciousness. He sure as hell couldn't move, a kind of sex-paralysis leaving his brains scrambled and his chest heaving like a racehorse after a hard run. He waited for some semblance of brain activity to return, watching Lacey's face.

Beside him on the king-size mattress and swimming in a sea of white linens, she appeared as dazed as him. Her cheeks flushed and her lips swollen from his kisses, she looked like a woman who'd just had incredible sex. Her blue eyes held a dreamy, far-off expression that made him wonder what she was thinking about. Was she already counting the ways he'd thrown off her dating profile? Or would she simply accept the joys of a vacation fling with someone wholly inappropriate?

Long moments passed before she finally spoke.

"Damon?"

"Hmm?" His attention snapped back to her face and he realized she'd lost that dreamy look.

"Do you really think I need to change hotels?" Worry crept into her voice.

She was thinking about Castine? The notion stirred an unexpected anger. Aw, hell. Make that jealousy.

He hated the idea of her wasting ten seconds thinking about another guy. Especially a dirtball that Damon knew damn well was running drugs into the States. The same kinds of drugs that had turned Damon's ex into an addict.

"It pays to be safe when you're dealing with a criminal." He untwined himself from her on the rumpled hotel mattress, needing some distance for a conversation that he hoped would be brief.

"Although he's not a proven felon yet, right?" Straightening, she pulled the sides of her cover-up together, shielding herself with the big white shirt. "Just an alleged criminal?"

"You're defending this guy?" He blinked his way out of the feel-good endorphin fog to make sense of what she was saying.

"Absolutely not. It's just demoralizing enough that my compatibility system chose a touch-happy jerk for me. Now I have to accept that the profiling also paired me with someone who might have violent tendencies and no ethics."

He couldn't understand her fast shift from sex to Castine, but told himself that at least she wasn't reading anything into what they'd just shared. Damon had been afraid she'd try and rope him into a deeper relationship that he wasn't ready for, but that hardly seemed to be something he needed to worry about. If anything he was more offended at how she could seemingly write off what had just happened without a backward glance.

"That's right. It's all about the profile for you, isn't it?"

"I'm a sociologist. I'm always interested in what motivates people to make choices in life." Shrugging, she retrieved the tie to her cover-up—the one she'd threatened to tie him up with—and threaded it around her waist. "I chose a career that lets me put those interests to work."

"So what are you going to do in town now that your dating prospect fell through?" He picked up his shirt and shoved his arms through the sleeves. "Did you leave any time in your schedule for a few days at the beach?"

Her eyes followed him as he dressed, the visual caress making him hot for her all over again.

"Yes. But since I can't blog about my dating experiences here, I decided to blog about the local singles scene in Puerto Rico for a special feature. I thought I'd try to visit some unusual places to draw extra traffic."

"Ah." He hated the idea of her hitting the nightspots on her own. What if Castine followed her? "For a woman who's no stranger to the clubs, I'm surprised you didn't know a few tricks for getting away from Castine's octopus hold last night."

"I didn't think I'd need to break out the jujitsu for a date that went through the system." She slid off the bed and retrieved a silver hairbrush from a nightstand.

"The all-mighty dating computer knows best," he muttered, stepping into his loafers.

"Could you be any more skeptical?"

"Not with my job." Buckling his belt, he met her clear blue gaze. "In my line of work I tend to see the worst side of human nature. The pirates and drug runners. The human traffickers. So I can't understand why an intelligent woman would take it on faith that some blind date she meets on foreign terrain is going be on the up-and-up. If you ask me, the only kind of guy who would use a service like that is looking for someone vulnerable anyhow."

"Excuse me?" She set down her hairbrush, her body going still inside the gauzy white cover-up she'd managed to keep on the whole time they'd been rolling around the bed.

Damon sensed the indignation in her voice, but he'd never hidden who he was, and he wouldn't start for the sake of a woman who left her dating decisions to the auspices of an electronic device.

"Face it, Lacey. The guys who hit up the dating services can't meet women on their own because they can't conform to the traditional system. They don't have the finesse or the patience to work through a woman's natural support systems of family and friends, so they take the easy way out and wait for a woman to be handed to them. That's the lazy approach. And if you ask me, that kind of guy isn't in it for meaningful conversation. He's there for a quick hook-up."

"I can't believe I just slept with a man who thinks so little of what I do." She fisted her hands and jammed them onto her hips, her body radiating pissed-off tension. "Actually, you're the only man I've slept with shortly after meeting, and I didn't meet you through a matchmaking service. As far as I can tell, that makes *you* the lazy one looking for an easy hook-up, not the guys I've been paired with by the computer who actually share things in common with me."

"Lacey—"

She lifted a hand to halt any interruption. Apparently she was only just warming up.

"No. I want you to hear me out. I came here to test out a new matchmaking system and I found a big freaking flaw, so I can hardly stand here and say my program is perfect. But I can tell you that I put it in place in an effort to avoid confrontations like this, where two people who don't understand each other at all are faced with wading through an awkward postcoital conversation because they jumped into a relationship based on absolutely nothing more than sexual attraction."

The fire in her eyes defied him to argue the point.

And really, how could he? He couldn't explain what drew them together any better than she could.

"Fair enough." He hated walking away from her like this, but he didn't know what to say, and he'd already done what he came here to do—ensure she knew to stay away from Castine. "For what it's worth, I think attraction occurs for a reason. Sometimes it's an indication that two people have things in common under the surface of sexual chemistry."

She quirked an eyebrow, standing her ground by the watercolor painting of a local seascape.

"But there has to be some effort by both parties to do that, don't you think? It's tough to find common ground when both sides come out swinging."

Had he done that?

He didn't want to think he'd pushed her away just for the hell of it—or for reasons he didn't really understand. But since he wasn't looking for a relationship anyhow and it never paid to let emotions get tangled up in anything work related, the wisest course of action would be to get out of her room before he did something incomprehensible like get her naked all over again.

Strangely, the impulse was there even while the air crackled with fighting words.

"Let me know if you need anything while you're down here." He brushed a quick kiss across her lips and then slowed himself, needing one last taste of her.

She pulled away. Cool. Ticked off.

"You'd better go."

"You'll find more nightlife in San Juan anyhow," he returned, trying to convince himself as much as her. He drew back, knowing a rebuff when he saw it.

Just as well, right?

But no matter how much space he put between him and Lacey Sutherland, he wouldn't be able to truly walk away until he knew for sure she was safe from whatever Nicholas Castine had in mind.

5

IF LACEY HAD BEEN a romantic, she might have thought the world seemed more beautiful in the wake of sex with Damon Craig. But it was only her body that felt marvelous in the aftermath.

Her brain? Not so much.

Her practical nature told her that the world was more beautiful today because she sat on one of the most gorgeous beaches on the globe on an island that boasted an average temperature of eighty-three degrees at this time of year. So the turquoise water sparkling in a protected natural pool at her feet was simply a product of fortuitous climate and geographical conditions. And the small rock formations that created the pool were merely a lovely happenstance that buffered Playa del Vega Baja from the Atlantic's enthusiastic waves.

She dug her toes deeper in the sand and told herself that it was nature making her skin flush with pleasure under the warm sun and sensitizing her erogenous zones to the caress of tropical breezes filtering through the nearby palm trees. It didn't have one damn thing to do with Damon Craig.

Or so she fervently hoped.

She would be going back home in a few days, while

the hot lieutenant would remain stationed right here. Too far away for a relationship that she hadn't been looking for anyhow.

Forcing her thoughts back to her planned visits to singles bars, Lacey worked on unique angles for each of the upcoming blog articles. Without knowing what the clubs had to offer, she wasn't sure what direction her content would take. But she hoped to touch on a gamut of issues for everyone from the romantics to the bedroom thrill seekers, all of whom converged on the singles scene every night. She needed something compelling since her idea for tracking her personal dating progress with Nicholas had fallen through in a big way.

A wet dog ran past her on the beach, a stick in its mouth from a game of fetch with its owner. Lacey watched it lay the prize at a young man's feet and thought about calling her sister.

Laura had become Lacey's counterpoint in her career, with a more free-wheeling perspective on dating that directly opposed hers and kept their debates lively. They'd always had a strained relationship, but the recent competition had made things both better and worse as the stakes had increased. Sure, they had a lot to discuss, but there were only so many paying clients to fuel both their businesses.

Somehow, Lacey didn't think the current dynamic was healthy for a sister-sister relationship any more than it would be good for a male-female relationship, but to bow out of the month-long contest now would make her look like a poor sport, since no one could deny she was coming up short in the satisfaction surveys.

Lacey was no closer to figuring out that X factor missing from her matchmaking program, the layer of chemistry that attracted people in addition to making them practical life partners. She had hoped her time in a hotel room with Damon Craig would teach her all she needed to know, but in spite of experiencing the heady stuff to the nth degree, she was no closer to pinning down the components for physical attraction.

People called it "chemistry" but there didn't seem to be one damn scientific thing about it.

"Would you like to buy a necklace, *señora?*"

A heavily accented voice startled Lacey from her thoughts and she turned to find a slim Puerto Rican woman with a knapsack on her shoulder and a fistful of simple, handmade jewelry.

"Um…" Lacey hesitated, tempted to buy something if only for the sake of distracting herself from her failing work and her frequent thoughts of Damon Craig. "I guess I'd better not."

The woman removed a pair of oversize sunglasses from her tanned face. "You are surrounded by beauty here. Why not remind yourself of your trip with something equally pretty?"

She lifted the fistful of semiprecious stones strung on leather thongs in a variety of colors. Turquoise and quartz mingled with shells and coral.

"I'm not really here on vacation," Lacey reasoned, thinking she'd already approached her trip to Puerto Rico a little too self-indulgently.

Memories of being pinned beneath a sexy Coastie fired across her synapses, burning the backs of her eyeballs with their heat.

The woman selling jewelry smiled. Kneeling down, she tucked the trinkets aside and settled herself in the sand.

"Then you have not discovered Puerto Rico." She extended her arm and made a sweeping gesture toward the pristine beach and brilliant, aquamarine water. "You have come to paradise, *señora*. Do not leave our shores without letting it touch you."

Lacey stilled inside for a moment, surprised to be taken to task by the jewelry woman. Determined to get back to her work in peace, Lacey reached for the merchant's necklaces. Maybe a purchase of something would quiet the pithy wisdom that echoed the same damn thing she'd heard from both her sister and Damon.

There were shells and beads, stones and little vials that appeared to contain powder or—blood? No. Probably some kind of herbal concoction to keep away bad spirits or some such. If she asked about it, the woman would surely launch into a long explanation. So Lacey picked up a pretty, simple piece that looked like a smooth, white rock.

"How about one of the white ones. How much for that?" She'd glimpsed the type of stone before, but had automatically denied herself, since she really wasn't a jewelry person. Her looks leaned more toward the average side and somehow, adorning herself with girly accessories had always struck her as a kind of false advertising.

"It is white turquoise. For you, twenty dollars." The slender woman picked through the necklaces, her fingers covered in silver rings. She wore a simple black tank top and jeans in spite of the heat. Her forearms were inked with intricate tattoos wherever her long hair didn't shield her skin.

"I'll take one." Lacey dug into her leather laptop bag, which she'd converted into a beach tote for the day. Bypassing her sunscreen and PDA, she found her wallet and withdrew a twenty.

"Gracias." The wandering saleslady took the bill but hesitated before handing over the necklace. "You will wear this and think of Puerto Rico, no?"

Lacey stifled a sigh. She'd surely remember the way a total stranger had swept her off her feet in ten seconds flat, making her whole life's work feel like a lie. How could she have had more dating success based on fate than on her new Connections system? The notion rankled even as it fueled her determination to do better. To put her years of study to work helping her clients.

"I will remember," she promised, ducking while the woman's ringed fingers lifted the necklace over Lacey's head to drop the brown leather thong into place.

"Good. I am Tatiana and if you ever return to the beach, I will make you a special necklace. Just for you." Rising to her feet, she plucked a small stone from a velvet pouch at her hip and handed it to Lacey. "This is my gift to you. A thank-you for buying my necklace. It is for good luck."

Lacey took the stone, a shiny bit of uncut quartz.

"I could use some good luck." She settled the stone on her beach blanket beside her and then tightened the leather thong on her necklace to shorten the cord. "Thank you, Tatiana."

"De nada. May paradise bring you many blessings." Smiling like a high priestess bestowing a benediction, the woman nodded before walking away, her flip-flops kicking up little clouds of sand as she hiked along the beach toward a cluster of teenage girls playing Frisbee.

Good luck and blessings? So far paradise had brought her a probable felon, a professional crisis and an unplanned sexual encounter with an intense man who had a major protector complex.

A man she never would have pegged for herself if she'd looked at their personalities on paper. But there was no denying she had the hots for Damon Craig. If she could find the formula for predicting what she'd found with Damon—a lust indicator to go along with the more substantive signs of compatibility—she'd generate more interest for Connections than her company had ever seen before.

Hell, she'd wipe her twin's intuitive, quasi-astrology system right off the map. And while that had never been her main goal, beating Laura had become a matter of professional self-preservation at this point.

Tucking her laptop back in her bag, Lacey picked up her quartz and wrapped it in a tissue before finding a slot for it inside her case. She'd never been the superstitious kind any more than she'd ever been a romantic. And yet, there was no denying her luck was about to change if she could only convince Damon to cooperate with her on this one last project.

Truth be told, she couldn't wait to see him again.

"THIS MISSION is going down the toilet and you're out good-timing with some chick you met at the bar?"

Damon knew his CO well enough to know this was not the time to break into his tirade to clarify details about yesterday's hotel encounter with Lacey. Somehow Commander Tom Stafford had heard about the events at Café Rosita's, probably thanks to the eternally mouthy Enrique, and was none too pleased that Damon had put himself in the line of fire with Nicholas Castine. And that he'd done so over a woman.

Damon had sat in on a DOG briefing on base that morning. Intel hadn't offered up anything new about the movement of drug shipments, so their unit was to continue routine flyovers of waters around Puerto Rico for now. But there were new reports of date-rape cases involving Castine's amnesia drugs around town, making everyone antsy to nail the guy for good. Damon especially.

After the meeting, Stafford had cornered him on the tarmac near the hangar where Damon's Dolphin—a short-range recovery helicopter—was housed. He was due for a recon mission of his own at fourteen hundred hours, and he needed to check over his aircraft.

"Care to explain why the hell you were in Rosita's at the same time as our team's primary target?" Stafford paused for air this time, indicating he was finally open to hearing a response.

In the distance, a chopper fired up for a routine mission over the Atlantic, the blades kicking up a soft breeze before they gathered speed. Other flyers on base did the routine stuff—the search and rescues, distress calls, shore patrol. Damon's unit was specially tasked to the drug-running operation, a mission that had been months in the planning. He would only be stationed here for as long as the threat remained, then it was on to wherever the DOG group was called next.

"The bar in question is a longtime Coast Guard hangout, sir. I saw at least four other guys from this base while I was there." Damon knew he wasn't supposed to live and breathe the operation, but he had a tough time leaving this one behind at the end of the day. Drug runners pushed his buttons to start with. And Castine had crossed a line when he'd started groping innocent women.

"And you figured you'd just blend right in. Is that it?" Stafford shook his head, his craggy, sea-worn face weathered beyond his forty-five years. But then, the guy had been a fisherman's kid before the Coast Guard. If rumor could be believed, the CO had been born shipboard during the roughest squall the Bering Strait had ever seen. He was one of those quiet types who rose through the ranks quickly, keeping to himself so much that his men were forced to fill in the blanks about his past.

He'd become a legend in his own time. A squinty-eyed, pissed-off legend at the moment, but a mythic presence nonetheless.

"We've never received orders to stay away from our target." In theory, Damon knew better than to argue, but he figured pointing out this fact might be important. He didn't want to be the guy assigned to his desk when the time came to bring Castine in.

"Common sense says not to get in a pissing match over a woman with a person of interest," Stafford returned, his steely gaze offering a warning more significant than the words he spoke.

"I thought at the time she might be involved in Castine's network." Damon knew no one in his unit would have complained if he'd brought forward a key contact to help further the mission. "But since she's clean—"

"We need to make sure she's not Castine's next target." The C.O. nodded, seemingly content that he'd been appropriately brought up to speed. "Just keep in mind you need to put the bigger mission above the call to play white knight. When this thing blows wide-open, I want you there to haul in this guy."

Stafford pivoted on his heel and stalked away, his crisp uniform impervious to the wind now blasting from the whipping copter blades.

Damon knew an order when he heard one, and this one kept him on unofficial guard duty for Lacey. He planned to make damn sure Castine never touched her again. The Coast Guard motto—Always Ready—was about to become his personal mantra where Lacey was concerned.

Before he headed to his chopper, he checked his cell-phone messages. Scrolling through the calls received, he knew several pertained to work items that could wait. But two calls were from a San Juan hotel he didn't recognize.

Lacey?

He checked his watch before jogging back inside the building that housed his temporary office to return the call. He'd left Lacey his direct number when they parted ways the day before, half-convinced he'd never hear from her again.

She'd been so incensed about his view of her work and—after hearing her side of it—he had to admit he could see her perspective better. Or, more accurately, he could at least appreciate that her fascination with compatibility was deeply rooted in a core belief that couples who shared each other's interests had better odds.

In theory.

But in his experience, it didn't pay to overanalyze relationship chemistry. You either had it, or you didn't. Then again, what did he know about a lasting relationship? His most serious girlfriend had ditched him for the thrills of illegal drugs.

The phone rang on the other end as Damon slipped into his office. He shared the space with two of his team members, but they were both out, giving him privacy.

"Hello?"

Lacey's voice smoothed over his senses, the mere sound of her an unexpected pleasure.

"It's Damon. You called?" He recognized the brusqueness of his approach, but damn it, she had a way of catching him off guard with her unique appeal.

"Oh. Um. Thanks for calling back." She paused and he heard some rustling around on the other end before she continued in a softer voice. "I found out something that might be of interest to you. Do you have time to meet with me tonight?"

He tensed, concern for her safety giving him a shot to the gut.

"I'll be tied up at the base until seven or so." He lowered his voice since he hadn't closed his office door. "Your, ah, former date didn't find you, did he?"

"No. But I found out something about him that might be helpful."

His mind ran at light speed with possible scenarios. Had they e-mailed? Did she have access to her company's computer files that could yield information about Castine?

"Stay away from him and I'll head over there after work. You're at the El San Juan?" He remembered the new hotel name from his call list since it had come up on caller ID.

"Yes. But I need to hit a nightspot tonight so I don't

fall behind on my blog feature." She paused. "I can't blow it off. I'm only in town four more days and I need to go for my research."

Great. He'd arrive just in time to see her sweet body poured into her clubbing clothes. And knowing what he did about the Puerto Rican nightlife, there was no way he'd be able to let her go out alone. Unprotected.

What if she ran into her date-deprived American businessman who was either a sex addict or a sexual predator or potentially both? If Nick Castine had trolled the Internet for women, Damon was damn sure the guy would at least give it a go on the local singles scene.

"I'll be there. Don't leave before you see me."

"*I* called *you,* didn't I?" She sighed on the other end of the phone. "Have I told you lately what a bossy sort of guy you are?"

He grinned, and that surprised him. No doubt about it, he enjoyed this woman on more than a physical plane.

"I do recall a conversation about my control issues. As I remember, that worked out pretty well for you last time."

Of course, it had paid off in spades for him, too. Just thinking about being with her spiked the temperature in the office.

"Yes, but that game's only fun to play when both parties can assume control on occasion." Her teasing tone didn't hide a hint of accusation.

And damn, but the temperature cooled at the re-minder of the trust issues he was in no position to resolve right now.

"Then I'll do my best to keep my hands off you." An idea he resisted as much as the thought of giving up control now and then. "But I think it was you who sabotaged my attempt to be a gentleman last time."

Another sigh.

"Don't make me regret calling you, Lieutenant Craig."

He could almost picture the threatening gleam in her eye. And oh man, he was in too deep too fast with this woman if he was already hearing the nuances of her tone.

"You won't," he promised himself as much as her. "I'll see you tonight. And, Lacey? Thank you for calling me."

Turning off the connection, he wondered what kind of information she might have for him. Would it be something that would move his mission forward? Or—and here's where his gut knotted—was it something that could put her in more danger?

Either way, he'd have a hard time getting his head back into the recon flight he had to report for soon. But was that because he wanted to take out Castine so badly he couldn't wait for any information that might nudge the mission along faster?

Or was it simply because he wanted to see Lacey Sutherland again so much it damn near hurt?

6

THE KNOCK SOUNDED on her door at 8:54.

Not that Lacey had been counting the moments until Damon's arrival or anything. Jeez. She was behaving like the kind of person Damon accused her clients of being—desperate. And wasn't that a cold splash of water to her fevered skin? She should still be torqued at him for what he'd said about her business instead of salivating at the mere thought of seeing him again.

Slowing her step as she neared the door of her new hotel room in San Juan, she forced herself to take a deep breath before she checked the peephole. Oh, mama. The uniformed man standing in her hallway was beyond delectable.

His dark green flight suit covered the lean, muscular body of a man who subjected it to intense physical labor. The expression on his face was focused, his lips compressed in a flat line, his eyes staring at the doorknob as if willing it to turn and remove the barrier between them.

Had she been taking deep breaths? They hadn't done jack squat to slow down her heart rate.

She hadn't planned on calling him again and subjecting herself to the powerful draw of their sexual attraction, as they had so little else in common. But the communication from Nick had left her no choice. Winging a prayer for restraint, she tugged open the door.

"Hi—" he started, his dark gaze raking over her body. "Sweet mother of— What the hell are you wearing?"

She looked down at her outfit, not sure she was seeing what he was seeing. A skirt. A tank top.

"They're clothes. My clubbing clothes to be precise. Why?" She patted her hips, suddenly paranoid her impulse dinner of cheese fries had gone directly to her glutes. When she'd lost forty pounds in college, she'd promised herself she would never let stress bite her in the butt that way again. "Don't tell me they don't fit anymore."

Sometimes she still didn't clothe her thinner body with the same finesse as women who'd been normal size their whole lives. She had to really work to bare any skin, and even then, she still usually covered up more than most women, her outfits leaning toward the conservative side.

He stepped deeper into her room and set down a duffel bag as he closed the door behind him.

"You can't go out like that." He took her elbow and pivoted her for a better view of her back half. "You can't even take the stairs in a skirt that short."

The way his eyes lingered on her thighs suggested maybe her butt hadn't doubled in size after all. The expression on his face appeared less horrified and more…lustful. And oh man, she couldn't afford to go down that road again. Not when Damon had such antiquated and borderline offensive beliefs about her work.

"Trust me, I know how to navigate stairs in this." The skirt wasn't even that short. "And while this is a little shorter than I usually wear, I can't go out to the kinds of places I'm headed tonight in my usual clothes or I'll never get past the doormen." She glanced back at his duffel bag. "I hope you weren't planning on moving in with me?"

It seemed a little presumptuous to bring an overnight bag to her room, but heaven help her, she'd probably given him the impression she would swoon at his feet anytime he showed his face within a mile radius of her.

Relinquishing her arm, he shook his head, still frowning about her clothes. "I didn't have time to change on base since I wanted to get over here." Unzipping the bag, he withdrew a pair of jeans, a black T-shirt and a black silk dress shirt. "So what did you find out?"

His fingers started working down the zipper of his flight suit past the Coast Guard insignia and some assorted patches.

Her mouth went dry as he unveiled square shoulders and chiseled abs covered by a thin white T-shirt. And then that was gone, too. Considering her legs and his torso, there was entirely too much bare skin in the room.

With an effort, she focused on relaying the information she'd called him about while he vanished into the bathroom. He left the door open so they could still talk.

"Castine left a note for me back at the Hotel Aquadilla. I didn't tell them where I was going when I checked out, obviously, but I called my former hotel today to see if anyone had left messages for me, since the abrupt departure."

If she peered into the bathroom, she could easily see him in the mirror. He slid on another shirt, leaving the top half of his flight suit hanging around his hips. He was completely covered now, but her brain supplied a mental video loop of his bare chest.

Not that she should be spying, damn it.

"And there was some communication from Castine?" He stilled, meeting her gaze in the mirror and grinning like he knew she'd been stealing peeks all along.

She looked away, her cheeks heating.

"Yes. It was a written note, not a phone call. I had the hotel in Aquadilla send it to my fax." She retrieved the paper she'd printed in the hotel business center and passed it to Damon in the bathroom. "Nick's signature is there, but I don't know if he took it to the hotel himself."

Damon's brows swooped together as he read the short missive: "In the Flesh is another singles' venue your blog readers might enjoy." Damon read the address aloud. "This is in Loiza. You're not seriously going to some nightspot *he* suggested."

"It was already on my list. And the last we knew, he was three hours away from here back in Aquadilla." She'd thought long and hard about it, but in the end, she didn't see any reason not to visit a public place. It wasn't as if Castine had suggested she check out some deserted dark alley. "Besides, if he's there, I'll have a cab take me the long way home to be sure he doesn't find me. Have you heard of this place?"

"Lacey, it's a sex club." He slid his arms into the silk shirt and left it open over the T-shirt. "You can't walk in there barely dressed. For that matter, you wouldn't want to go in there wearing combat boots and a flak jacket."

"You're right about the combat boots. Too S & M-looking."

Damon cursed a blue streak that made her smile. Who knew she had the power to torment him so easily?

"I'm going," she informed him in no uncertain terms, determined to make sure he understood she wouldn't be swayed by his he-man tactics anymore. Plenty of jobs besides military and law enforcement came with a bit of danger. Journalists' research took them to less than ideal places. And, damn it, she was going to do her research. "You don't have to like it, but I am writing an article on this place regardless. I thought you would appreciate the tip about this guy since it seemed curious to me that he recommended a club on the northeast side of the island near San Juan when we last saw him on the northwestern corner, a few hours away."

"Maybe he's telling you he knows where you're staying." He slipped off his shoes and speared his fingers into his close-shorn hair, an exasperated gesture. "Shit. You should not set foot in there."

"I think it's more likely he remembers me saying I was going to check out some clubs closer to San Juan during the week. I e-mailed him a few times before I came down here, and he knows about my work for Connections. The fact that I'm checking out unusual singles' venues is a matter of public record." She picked up the piece of quartz crystal Tatiana had given her and slid it into her purse, figuring she could use every bit of luck she could get tonight.

Damon's low whistle alerted her to his watchful gaze, and she felt awkward for primping in front of him. She forgot to be self-conscious when he reached for his zipper to unfasten the rest of the flight suit, however.

"What are you doing?" Warmth flooded her veins at that simple act full of so much masculine promise. Her body responded in ten different ways from her aching breasts to her quivering thighs and a whole host of destinations in between.

"Changing. Remember?"

Flustered, she turned around, leaving him alone to finish dressing.

"Don't leave on my account," he called from the bathroom.

A minute later he emerged wearing a pair of jeans and stuffing his flight suit into his bag.

"I'm going with you, okay? If you're dead set on going to this place, I really need to be with you to make sure no one hassles you." He appeared completely serious, his face settling into grave lines.

"You have a protector complex of gargantuan proportions, you know that?" She shook her head in disbelief, her hair swinging softly against her neck with the motion.

The thought made her realize how sensitive her skin had become since he'd entered the room. Or more precisely, since he'd taken off his flight suit.

"Only for women I've rescued and then proceeded to sleep with." A grin kicked up one corner of his mouth, stretching that dimple on his chin into a more subtle depression.

"That must keep you awfully busy." She couldn't keep her eyes off his mouth.

"Not since you're the only woman who fits the description." He stared at her for a long moment, and for a second she thought he might lean closer for a kiss. But he only caressed her with his eyes until he spoke again. "Do you have any idea what you're getting into at In the Flesh, by the way?"

The shift in the direction of their conversation unbalanced her, and she found herself disappointed that he hadn't kissed her. She'd been so sure he was thinking about it.

Trying to focus on what he was saying about the club on tonight's list, she hoped she'd be able to recall the information later for the next article in her series, since her thoughts were a long way from business right now.

SHE HADN'T KNOWN what she was getting into.

That much was patently obvious to Damon as they wound their way through the maze of halls at the old paper mill converted into a luxury watering hole for fetishists and exhibitionists, voyeurs and purveyors of the S & M scene. The expression on Lacey's face as they passed a man on a leash said it all. She might have researched the singles' scene before, but not *this* singles' scene. She gripped his arm tighter as they walked by a topless woman sporting elaborate nipple rings bearing long chains that led to her boyfriend's arm torque and clamped to the silver band with a padlock.

Damon hoped the guy didn't need to throw any punches in an impromptu bar fight or he'd inflict a hell of a lot of hurt on the poor girl's breasts.

"I didn't picture this," Lacey admitted as they wove around another set of velvet ropes, admitting them to the second-floor gallery overlooking the dance floor.

The place was decked out in blue-and-black zebra wallpaper, an eighties decorating nightmare. There were mirrors on the ceilings and small disco balls suspended at regular intervals, giving the club a psychedelic atmosphere.

"It's not too late to get out of here." Personally,

Damon couldn't wait. The weirdos this sort of place attracted gave him the creeps. Sure, there were some regular Joes just out searching for a thrill, and they didn't bother him. It was the nipple rings with chains, the carnival barkers trying to get patrons off into the side rooms to view more explicit entertainment and the hardened look of the lap dancers who'd seen everything by the time they were…twenty-one? He sure as hell hoped those women were twenty-one, but some of them appeared damn young to him.

Not that he'd been to this club many times. It was only on his radar since it was used for bachelor parties or as a destination to show newcomers to Borinquen. But even though he hadn't been to In the Flesh often, he knew the type of establishments from being stationed all over. Sex clubs were the updated version of strip joints, with more to see, more to do and more ways to feed diverse sexual appetites.

"I don't want to leave," Lacey insisted, speaking close to his ear since the music vibrated at a deafening volume. "If I've been deceiving myself about what people in the dating world want, I damn well need to face facts. I didn't even know places like this existed."

She left his side to position herself at the rail overlooking the dance floor. He followed close on her heels, determined not to lose sight of her among the sexual thrill seekers and jaded clubbers who'd seen everything. Done everything. The crowd that populated the place would think nothing of sweeping a neophyte into one of the back rooms for a "welcome" to the club scene. Lacey could be drugged and violated in ten minutes flat. And—depending on what types of drugs were used—she might not even remember it. Was that why Castine had invited her here?

Damon kept an eye on the shadows while sticking close to Lacey. By the rail overlooking the dance floor, she watched in fascination at the mass, near orgy among the partygoers. Overt sex acts were confined to back rooms, so there wasn't anything supergraphic going on under the strobe lights. But there were more topless women here, some of whom were dancing with their hands all over each other—or with any man in reach. At the four corners of the floor, professional dancers were stationed on raised platforms above the crowd. They were the only ones who were completely naked.

The girl on the northernmost platform gyrated with what looked like a python wrapped around her and surrounded by candles and torches. Two of the other professionals used poles in a more traditional, stripper-style approach. The fourth woman had been greased up and painted with some kind of shiny blue substance. The only areas that maintained the traditional flesh color were her breasts and her shaved cooch.

"Condom?" a feminine voice asked over his shoulder.

He turned at the same time Lacey did, and a thin redhead with an unnaturally huge rack carried a tray full of prophylactics and a few small sex toys like an old-time cigarette girl. She wore a short skirt and a low-cut blouse in the French-maid style except that the outfit was pink and black.

"Do these really work?" Lacey reached right into the tray and came up with a seriously studded cock ring. The package promised the wearer could bring his partner to orgasm within five minutes or less…among other things.

The girl grinned and kept her eyes on Damon.

"If your partner knows how to wear one they do."

Lacey huffed an incensed sort of sound as she tossed the toy back onto the tray.

"I asked you a legitimate question and it wasn't to flirt with my man." She narrowed her eyes at the redhead and gave her an eat-shit-and-die stare. "You just lost yourself a sale."

The other woman frowned.

"Suit yourself. I wouldn't buy any toys if I had a partner like this one at the controls." She winked at him before turning on her heel, boobs bouncing. "Enjoy yourselves."

Damon turned back to Lacey in time to see a waiter carry a tray full of phallus-shaped glasses toward a table of noisy women nearby. He didn't know how many more sex references one man could handle, but he had a good idea he wouldn't last long at In the Flesh at this rate.

"The nerve of some people," Lacey muttered, her gaze following the milky white drinks the waiter doled out to the lady patrons.

"You held your own," Damon assured her, still surprised and, yeah, sort of stoked that Lacey had referred to him as "my man."

Not that he was ready to delve into any kind of relationship. He'd seen too many military affairs go up in flames—his own included—to try to navigate that particular land mine again. Besides, Lacey had made it clear she didn't see the potential for long-term compatibility. She was as surprised they'd connected as he was.

"Yes, but I chased off someone who could have been a good source for the blog column I need to write about this place." She turned away from the dance floor to study the slightly more sedate crowd in the upper gallery. "Who am I going to hit up for a quickie interview now? The guy in the corner trying to chat up the hot blonde who won't look at him? Or the fake lesbians mauling each other against the bar in an effort to attract men?"

Damon couldn't help it. His head whipped around at that one. Too bad he didn't see any such thing near the bar. Lacey laughed. "Got ya."

Keyed up from the atmosphere and from the sight of Lacey in her tiny miniskirt and miles of bare legs, Damon reached for her and pulled her to him. "Are you sure you want to tease a man whose restraint is being tested every second tonight?"

He was tense from watching out for her, tense from keeping a lock on a hunger for her that kept growing no matter how he tried to ignore it.

"You wanted to come with me," she reminded him, her high, small breasts pressing against his chest with each rapid breath she took.

He tunneled his hand a scant inch under her tank top to feel a hint of bare skin at her back. Warm and silky.

"And I want to come with you more every second we spend here. Let's go somewhere more private now that you've seen this place." He hadn't intended to flirt with her, let alone make obvious come-ons when he was supposed to be here to protect her. To make sure Castine hadn't set a trap for her.

But with Castine's drug shipment due in this week and his last confirmed sighting a three-hour drive away, Damon relaxed his guard long enough to touch her. Castine hadn't gotten this far in his illegal business by ignoring the details when big transactions were under way. He'd be a fool to spend time chasing Lacey around when he had a multi-million-dollar delivery to oversee.

Besides, there was something undeniably sensual about Lacey, some spark of latent adventurousness beneath her uptight, workaholic tendencies.

As a man who'd buried himself in his job to the detriment of one relationship after another, he couldn't help but identify with her dedication to her work. Admire her grit and belief even if he didn't buy in to the whole matchmaking thing himself. Watching her scientific brain trying to analyze the defining social characteristics of singles in this over-the-top scene only gave him one more reason to be fascinated by her.

And that, coupled with a physical attraction unlike anything he'd ever experienced, was making it damn hard for him to keep his hands off her.

IT SEEMED Little Miss Traditional Girl wasn't as pure and reserved as she once pretended.

Nick Castine sat in a back room at In the Flesh, watching Lacey Sutherland via a two-way mirror. The club had all kinds of back rooms, from private places for a lap dance to modified hotel-style rooms that could be rented by the hour. Nick had used both of them in the past, but tonight he'd simply wanted a place to observe Lacey without G.I. Joe spotting him. He'd already arranged for her date to be intercepted and Lacey to be brought back here to him. Their car was being staked out even now so they couldn't slip away without him knowing.

Nick couldn't really afford the time away from his current operation. His biggest shipment ever was due for arriving just south of the Gulf and he needed to be available to make sure the load was properly divided into a variety of smaller vessels for easier penetration through an ever-tightening Coast Guard presence. But Lacey Sutherland's calling him a lowlife in Café Rosita's was a tale that had spread to some of the key players in his organization. He needed to avenge her blatant put-down. And he would make damn sure his vengeance went further than just banging her in a club back room.

So here he was. Watching the unsuspecting woman while she allowed her new boyfriend—one Lieutenant Damon Craig, if his informants could be trusted—to touch her like they were already lovers. The man's hands slipped under her clothing when he thought no one watched. And far from squirming away, Lacey practically quivered at the touch. Even from Nick's vantage point, he could see her rapt attention on the Coastie, her eyes never leaving his for long.

"Excuse me." Some butt-kissing club staffer interrupted his thoughts, her scanty outfit marking her as one of the so-called concierge people. Nick knew they filled other roles, as well, since this one had personally lifted her skirt for him on two occasions. "We seem to be all out of the pills you wanted, Mr. Castine. Is there anything else I can get for you?"

She shifted her hips suggestively, as if the offer of her body would make up for the club owner's carelessness with the stash Nick had supplied him. They had a long-standing deal to help one another out, supply each other's addictions where possible.

But this was inexcusable. The amount of drugs he fed this place kept patrons buying drinks and paying ridiculous cover charges at this rat hole of a bar. And the Special K was his drug of choice for this kind of thing. No sex tricks from a woman he'd already had before would take the place of what he needed from Lacey.

"Fine," Nick tossed off as agreeably as possible, unwilling to let his frustrations show. "Give her the alternative. But you can let your boss know I'm not happy with how he's managing the supply. Understand?"

He was wired. Tense. Pissed. A deadly combination if these people couldn't provide him with better service. He would have to use the Rohypnol tonight, and that irritated the hell out of him. There were subtle differences in the drugs, and Nick had experienced more intriguing results with Ketamine. Special K didn't just wipe out the memory of the sex act afterward, it also added a level of pleasure during sex by diminishing the ability to fight back. Nick enjoyed watching women struggle with that, the forced submissiveness a cherished component of the act for him.

His plan-B drug didn't give his partners as much clarity. Or fear.

"Actually, Mr. Castine, we appear to be out of that, too, unless you have a personal stock?" The girl folded her arms across her barely clad breasts, her flirting finished now that she saw Nick didn't want her tonight. She delivered her shitty news with zero understanding of what it meant to him.

The stupid chick acted as if the bankrupt cupboard shelves were no big deal, while Nick silently seethed with the need to have Lacey.

"Personal stock?" Rage spun up inside him so fast he didn't have a chance of holding it back. Rising from his chair, he realized the girl was finally getting a clue that she'd crossed a line.

Good. He let his fist fly, unable to call it back into a more appropriate open-handed slap. After all, this was a chick and not some steely jawed South American drug maker.

As he watched the girl hit the opposite wall, her slender body propelled by just one punch, Nick realized he needed to ease up. Not that he gave a shit what the club owner thought. But he couldn't afford to leave a trail the way he had once before. He'd worked his ass off to be sure no one pressed charges last time.

He *had* to get himself under control.

"Listen to me, sweetheart." He held out his hand and helped the girl up while she clutched the side of her face. At least there was no blood. "Go give the bitch whatever we have. I don't care if it's strychnine or a double shot of Jack Daniels. But I damn well came for the show. Do you understand me?"

The girl whimpered something that might have been a yes before she managed to say, "I'll give her the X. I know he's got some of that left over."

"Fine." Nick ushered the girl toward the door, stuffing a fifty in her bra for her trouble. "Get it in her next drink for me, and I'll take good care of you next time I come in."

Returning his attention to the two-way mirror, Nick kept his focus on Lacey. She swung her hips in a teasing, delectable dance. And while a shot of Ecstasy wasn't going to make her as pliable as he would like, it could easily ratchet up her need to unbearable levels. When a woman wanted sex that badly, there was no telling what lengths she might go to in order to have it.

Especially when her he-man bodyguard would very shortly be…indisposed. Unable to protect her, let alone provide what she wanted most. Nick had done some preliminary checking into Damon Craig's background and discovered a few interesting facts—connections Nick could leverage to be sure Craig was distracted tonight.

Just the thought of it sent a wave of calm through him, soothing the frayed edges of his hunger. Lacey might be one of many, many women he'd sought in the last few months, but the matchmaker compelled him. Perhaps because she'd gotten away from him so easily the first time. But also because of her job. She specialized in putting men and women together and, to a certain extent, so did he.

He wanted to know all about what drew women to men. What made them eager to shed their panties. Lacey had to understand those dynamics to be in her business and he wanted her to share her secrets with him, to help him in finding one woman after another to satisfy the beast in him that could never be appeased with just one.

Besides, seeing how sexually open she was tonight after she'd given him the cold shoulder on their date was an issue he wanted to address with her. She'd made herself out to be someone traditional, someone who wanted to be romanced. But she'd relinquished those values for the guy with the hand up her blouse right now, that was for damn sure.

She'd changed her tune in a hurry for the U.S. military man, and that made Nick feel cheated.

No woman teased him and got away with it.

7

LACEY'S BID FOR RESTRAINT with Damon was all but forgotten inside the walls of the sex club.

Even if leather clothes and studded toys weren't her thing, she couldn't help the flash of arousal at being around people who gave sex so much prominence in their lives. The club practically oozed the pheromones of people whose urges were close to the surface. People who took the physical aspect of sex damn seriously.

All of which only enhanced her desire to peel off Damon's clothes and crawl around a bed with him. Especially when he grabbed her by the waist and told her he wanted to go somewhere private.

Pass the smelling salts, please. This man would have her in a dead faint if he kept this up.

"I don't think—" She cleared her throat that had gone bone-dry. "That is, I can't go anywhere with you until I finish up here." Although she had the feeling if she walked out the door with him right now he would have her hurtling toward release seconds after they found a private place.

But no matter how much she wanted him, her work came first. Her job had been there for her in the past when she'd needed to rebuild her self-confidence. It had bolstered her through her mother's unwillingness to recognize what creeps she married, her sister's competitiveness and her own insecurities that she'd worked hard to shake. Her work would be there for her when this sexy hunk of a man disappeared from her life next week. So she wouldn't ignore it now.

"How can I help?" He skimmed his hand along the waistband of her skirt, never dipping beneath it, his fingers tracing small circles along her spine. "I want us to get out of here as fast as humanly possible. I don't see any direct threats, but I've got a bad feeling about this place."

He peered around the perimeter, and she wondered if he still thought Nick Castine had followed her here. Unfortunately her job made her work public enough that she couldn't hide from every creep whose match didn't work out. She'd learned a long time ago you couldn't dig a hole and hide in it when life scared the crap out of you. As long as she was smart and cautious, she wouldn't ever live in the shadows again.

"I need some informal interviews." She reached in her purse. "I'm happy to buy free drinks for anyone willing to speak—"

He held up a hand to halt her words.

"Keep it. I don't think I'll have any trouble rounding up people to talk to you." His jaw twitched restlessly with the sentiment. "You want to find a spot to sit down, and I'll start sending sexual deviants your way?"

Nodding, she hoped she could discover something meaningful from these interviews while under the influence of a sex drive humming along at hyperspeed.

"I'll sit right here, but if you could go easy on the

deviants and steer more normal, relatable people in my direction, I'd appreciate it." She needed to write something edgy for her dating blog, but not so out there that her readers wouldn't relate.

What readers? a small voice in the back of her brain asked. Her visitor hits had been dropping for months.

Snagging a chair at a table two men and a woman had just vacated, Lacey watched the curvy brunette walk away with an adoring-looking stud on each arm. Curious how a woman handled two men when Lacey could hardly manage one. Well, she could imagine handling the sex. It was the idea of morning-after conversation with not one but two guys ready to do the can't-commit dash that stymied her.

A man's whistle interrupted her musings and she turned to see Damon watching her, a dark scowl on his face.

"Don't tell me the relationship guru is interested in a three-way." He stood not two feet from her, but his voice turned the heads of at least a half-dozen people nearby.

Embarrassment crawled over her skin in a heated flush.

But damn it, why should she be embarrassed? She wasn't the one walking around a club in nipple rings and assless chaps.

"Oh, please. Like it's never crossed your mind before?" She withdrew a pad of paper and a fountain pen from her purse and did her best to appear unfazed.

His scowl deepened as more than a few club-goers appeared interested in the conversation. A couple of girls and a nearby guy leaned closer to hear.

An opportunity she could hardly pass up, considering her need for blog material.

"Would you like to have a seat?" Lacey offered,

waving her paper at them to prevent misunderstandings. "I'm doing an article on the local singles' scene if you have time for a couple of questions."

The guy dropped into the metal chair so fast you'd think he was carrying magnets in his back pocket. The girls followed suit, putting their fruity-looking drinks on the table before lowering themselves more slowly into the other chairs.

And—how flipping perfect—Lacey realized they were twins. Not like her and Laura with more differences than similarities. These two were identical.

Damon stepped closer, leaning down to eye level with her before she could begin.

"I hope you know I work alone." He spoke to her, but he made damn sure the guy seated across the table from her heard every word.

The unmistakable sexual heat in his eyes sizzled through her skin. The raw potency of his claim made her itchy to leave with him and see what kind of follow-through he'd deliver on those words.

"Then I hope you're willing to pull a double shift, Lieutenant."

DAMON HAD TO GET out of there.

He breathed in the night air near the back door of the club, his eyes never leaving Lacey where she still sat at the same table, interviewing people about their dating preferences.

At first he'd just been overheated by the whole three-way conversation. After her teasing words, he wanted to take her away from the club and have her underneath him to wipe out any thought from her head of any other guy.

But he had a job to do. Somehow Lacey Sutherland had an in with a drug smuggler, a connection he needed to keep tabs on in order to protect her and—on a practical note—to help keep tabs on Castine. That job hadn't driven him in search of fresh air though. Nor had the steamy atmosphere.

Watching her work, however, was killing him. Interview subjects came and went, and he'd weathered every conversation she had with them from toe fetishes to voyeurism. What got under his skin were the relationship questions.

Lacey was relentless but subtle with each interview subject as she turned every conversation back to deeper intimacy. How did they feel about long-term relationships? Were they really looking for quick sexual fulfillment or were they open to real love?

At first the guys especially tended to toss off some disposable answer to the more meaningful questions. Damon could have scripted their predictable responses himself.

Yet Lacey had been as dogged as Barbara Walters in pursuit of tears and truth. She'd persisted with questions about past broken hearts or their first loves, and suddenly she'd turn the slickest of Casanovas into sensitive guys who'd been burned and really wanted to find someone who loved and accepted them.

And that had Damon sprinting to the exit.

He'd gotten over Kelly, but he didn't want to think about how much the aftermath had cost him. He'd thought she was special because she'd practically followed him to the ends of the earth by tagging along on his Alaskan stint. They'd met in Seattle on one of his weekends off, fallen into bed together and were never apart again. At least not until she'd pulled the same stunt with another guy.

He stood at the back exit now, propping the door open for partyers who came out to smoke or dance in the alley where a night breeze off the ocean made it cooler. Lacey remained well within his sights, her straight posture and scholarly scribbling setting her apart from a club full of people who just wanted to get busy for the night.

Or, Lacey had revealed, people who *thought* they just wanted to get busy. Apparently even the most jaded of sex-club-goers wanted to find true love one day. If not with the horny set of twins he or she brought home from the disco, then with someone else sometime in the future.

The whole thing hit a little too close to home.

"You need a cigarette?" someone asked him in Spanish, a skinny brunette covered in tatts with hair down to her butt. She wore a dark blazer in spite of the heat and she parted it now to show him a breast pocket full of joints.

Professional interest stirred. Was this chick a bottom feeder who only sold for enough cash to support her own habit? Or could she be higher up the food chain?

"Do you have anything stronger? My girl and I want to have a good time tonight." He grinned at her, hoping to score a lead on the sex drugs infiltrating U.S. waters.

"Don't we all?" She winked at him as she brushed past him into the club. "But I hear you have to know someone to find that kind of stuff. Good luck, *guapo*."

Crap. How come *he* had to know someone while his ex had had no trouble morphing from a law-abiding, sweet girl into a druggie in a matter of weeks?

His cell phone rang and he flipped it open, expecting to see Enrique's number or someone from work. The area code didn't help—a 520 number was listed along with a phone company.

"Craig here." He had to shout over the music since even out here, the reggaeton thumped with a bass line to make a man go deaf.

"Damon?"

The soft feminine voice on the other end was no louder than a whisper, but something about the tone and accent of the word, an indefinable speed and pitch, clued him in to the caller's ID.

"Kelly?" Straightening, he stared back into the club to see Lacey tipping her soda to her lips while her interview subject spoke. Something about the phone call felt disloyal to Lacey even though they'd only just met.

And what the hell did his former girlfriend want with him after all this time?

"Do you have a minute?" she asked while he thumbed the volume switch on the phone so he had a chance of hearing her. "I've got some information your group might be interested in."

Instantly alert, he wondered if she'd gotten clean. She knew about his affiliation with the drug op, a specially coordinated mission that he'd started preparing for last year.

"What kind of information?" He wouldn't play games with her just because she wanted to talk.

"Can I reach you on a landline?" She sounded nervous, her words rushed. "It's important."

What the hell could she know that would be relevant to his job? Possibilities spun around his head. If she was clean, there was a chance she had learned something.

She was sharp, her work in research and development for a plastics manufacturer the kind of job that required brains. Maybe feeding her own drug habit had put her in the path of bigger dealers.

"How about tomorrow?" He needed to focus right now. With Lacey still on the loose in a sex club Castine had directed her to, he had to concentrate on keeping her safe. "I can call you from work."

"No," she protested, her connection breaking up so he couldn't hear what followed.

Barely able to make out half of what she said, Damon assured her he would call her back the next day and then hung up.

Peering back into the club, he saw Lacey's last interview subject was gone and the brunette with the ink who had attempted to sell him a joint was leaning down to speak to her. Was Lacey trying to interview her, too? Or did the pot-pusher see Lacey as a prospective user?

Irritated at the idea of dealers trying to flip good people, Damon shoved his phone into his pocket and charged through the side door into the club. The scent of sweat and beer mingled with a hundred different perfumes, the heat intensifying all the smells into a ripe mix.

A few yards away, Lacey laughed at something the dealer said, her whole face animated as she tipped sideways in her chair and clutched her sides. Curious, Damon hastened his pace. He didn't see Lacey as the kind of woman to pick up a recreational joint during a night out, but then again, how well did he know her?

Shit. Maybe he should have taken one of Lacey's damn compatibility tests to see how they matched up. He sure hadn't called it right with Kelly.

"Almost ready, Lace?" he asked as he reached her table. For reasons he didn't fully understand, he put his arm around her. Claimed her in front of the drug dealer, the waitress delivering Lacey's next soda and the DJ in a booth right behind them.

"Sure," she agreed, rising to her feet as she dumped her pad of paper and pen back into her purse. "Tatiana, this is Damon. Damon, Tatiana."

"You two know each other?" He tried to hide his surprise.

Had Lacey trod deeper into Nick Castine's world than she'd let on? Clearly Castine wasn't the only person she knew around town with connections in the drug community. Suspicions doused his hunger for her with a cold splash of caution.

"Tatiana was selling necklaces at Playa del Vega Baja when I went to the beach earlier this week." Lacey turned to the woman and smiled. "She sells beautiful things."

"Only the best." Tatiana winked at him. "I'm sorry I could not provide what you wanted this evening."

The petite dealer melted into the crowd, the mermaid tattoo on the back of her shoulder blowing them a kiss before she disappeared completely.

"I'd ask what she wanted to provide for you, but I really need to get out of here." Lacey's voice held a worried note he'd never heard before.

"Are you okay?" He scanned the people around her, seeking out anyone who might have upset her without him noticing. He wanted to get out of here. Now.

"No." She wavered on sky-high heels that laced up her ankles with big silk roses centered on the buckles. "I feel strange. Kind of buzzed, but I haven't been drinking."

His instincts tingled a warning along the back of his neck as he reached out to steady her.

"How so?" He picked up the glass of soda a waitress had delivered to her a few moments before. Sniffing the contents, he studied the liquid for cloudiness. "Describe exactly what you're feeling."

The Coast Guard's frequent drug-interdiction missions had given him plenty of training in recognizing the signs of a wide variety of substance abuses. The LSD users went ape shit when they couldn't handle the hallucinations, the pot smokers turned red-eyed and mellow, and the coke sniffers attempted to conquer the world in their manic marathons of no sleep.

Lacey's glass didn't reveal any hints of a drug, but that didn't mean it wasn't there. It could have easily been slipped into a previous glass in a moment when neither of them had been watching. He'd been keeping an eye out for Nick Castine to show up tonight, wary of his involvement in steering Lacey toward this particular club, so Damon's vigilance at watching over her had suffered from his divided attention.

And, damn it, why had Kelly called him tonight of all times?

Lacey leaned more heavily on him, her slender body molding to his with an abandon he'd bet she'd never demonstrate in public if not for the effects of some kind of drug.

Crap. He tried to nudge her toward an exit, but in the crush, he didn't make much headway. Stopping, he tried to do a quick evaluation of her symptoms so he knew what they were dealing with.

"I'm kind of dizzy. But really sensitive, like my skin is prickly." She rubbed her thigh against his in an overt request that brought his sex drive raging back to life in spite of all circumstances that should have made him careful. Wary. "*Really* sensitive."

Apparently the sight of her wrapped around him appealed to the voyeurs in the club because they were quickly attracting an audience. A handful of single men turned to watch the hemline of Lacey's short skirt as she wound her leg around his, tilting her hips into him. A guy nearby groaned at the sight while a tall transvestite shouted encouraging catcalls.

Damon scouted the perimeter for the nearest place to go for privacy since the closest exit out to the main street seemed worlds away. There was no way this hole-in-the-wall place would meet a building inspector's code.

"That's it, honey. Work it for your man!" The she-male dressed in a green-sequined gown and rhinestone tiara put two fingers in her mouth and whistled.

Damon, in the meantime, tried to juggle Lacey and the drink that needed to be tested at a lab. No easy feat when Lacey was hell-bent on kissing him, her fingers walking up his chest to tunnel between the buttons on his shirt.

More whistles.

Damn.

"Lacey." He pulled back from her just enough to break contact at the lips since he guessed she might fall over if he let go of her completely. "We need to go someplace private for this, okay?"

He looked into her eyes and saw her pupils dilated as wide as a doll's. She blinked without comprehension and her gaze dipped back to his mouth. Lingered.

"I want you," she whispered, her tongue darting out to moisten her lips.

He felt the swirl of her pink tongue as keenly as if it had connected with his skin. He throbbed in time with the incessant club music, his blood hammering with needs he had to suppress. He had no idea how much of the drug she'd been given or even what kind of drug it had been, although his early guess would have to be a stimulant.

"Did you take any drugs, Lacey?" He had to ask, had to know. If there was any chance she did this to herself or if—his jaw clenched—she was somehow involved with this ring of drug importers, after all, he would be furious.

"Drugs?" The very idea seemed to confound her, her brow wrinkling in slow motion since her reaction times were way off. "I've never touched a medication that wasn't prescribed for me."

As he felt for her pulse at her wrist, she trailed her hand lower down the front of his shirt, hooking on his belt buckle for a moment before smoothing over the clasp with a deliberate, teasing motion.

"Excuse me," a woman's voice intruded before he finished out his count of heartbeats per minute, although he already knew the number was elevated.

He turned to see the busty redhead in charge of condom sales. Her tray full of prophylactics and sex toys glittered like a forbidden treasure trove to a man who couldn't possibly indulge himself right now. He prayed Lacey wouldn't notice the bedroom bounty or she might help herself and start undressing.

"We're all set, but thanks." Damon hoped she would disappear so he could make it to the bathrooms and splash some cold water on Lacey's face, but the saucy condom wench jammed a foil packet in his shirt.

"This one's on the house for putting on such a good

show for my customers. Your theatrics are turning on the whole place." She gestured to the gallery above where another crop of onlookers watched Lacey's antics in rapt interest.

Only now did Damon notice the strap of her tank top had fallen and the cotton fabric of her shirt had slid down to her breast, exposing a hot-pink bra studded with crystals that spelled out "Sexy." He'd been so focused on her pulse, he hadn't noticed that she was falling out of her clothes.

Of course, the voyeurs on the upper deck probably had a prime view of the taut nipple ready to emerge from the bra at any second. Could he suck as a protector any more than he already did?

Wrenching the tank top back into place, Damon turned Lacey away from him so that they stood side by side with her pressed tight against him. Enough was enough.

"We're leaving now." Damon brushed past the condom saleslady with Lacey in tow, the drink sloshing over the sides of the cheap bar glass as he edged around dancers and waitresses, sex-crazed patrons and leather-clad S & M fans.

"But we have rooms available," the condom girl called, her throaty voice penetrating the noise of reggaeton and shouted conversations. "You don't have to leave to put that protection to use."

Damon paused for a moment, half considering the idea since he didn't know how he'd make it all the way back to the El San Juan Hotel with Lacey wrapped around him like a wet suit. Besides, if this was truly her first trip, the effects would be stronger. Harder. All the more difficult to ignore in public.

Then reason kicked him squarely in the ass. The only place he was going right now was the E.R. That condom in his pocket would damn well wait until Lacey was under a doctor's care and the glass she'd drunk from was in a lab being tested for every possible drug.

"Thanks, but no thanks." He steeled himself against Lacey's bump and grind against him, knowing he'd have to make a scene to get her out of here. "We're leaving."

Lifting her off her feet, he kissed her because he couldn't fight her advances while juggling her and the tainted glass as he plowed through the crowd. The hail of whistles from half-dressed club-goers made him angry when the woman in his arms was suffering from a drug trip that could go bad at any moment. Reaching the street, he was halfway to his car when he saw two souped-up black Hummers parked on either side of his ride.

A coincidence?

Not in a million years.

This was Puerto Rico, not Manhattan or Miami where plenty of average Joes drove the same make and model, tacky gold mag wheels and all.

Taking a step back toward the club, he hid in the shadows while Lacey moaned in his arms.

"Shh." He hushed her with a kiss, all the while keeping his eyes on those two ominous vehicles.

If they'd been in San Juan, he would have simply taken her somewhere else. He could have dashed into any public restaurant or bodega and called for a cab.

But this was Loiza, a small beach community that prided itself on its undeveloped shoreline and the lack of tourist traps. It sprawled over a stretch of rocky coast accessible by a tiny road over a one-lane bridge on the east side of the island. There were no streetlamps here, let alone paved streets. The sex club sat on a property that wasn't much better than an ancient beach shack, despite its two floors. People parked their cars on nearby hilly sand dunes to attend.

Damon had nowhere to run except back inside.

"Aren't you going to take me somewhere?" Lacey asked, her voice a warm, breathy sigh against his ear.

"Sure I am." He would have to call for reinforcements, but until the cavalry arrived, he planned to stay in the thick of things, planting them firmly inside a building packed to the gills with people. Potential witnesses if Castine was stupid enough to try anything here. "We're going to get ourselves a private room."

8

TWO HOURS LATER Lacey was going out of her mind in a private back room at the sex club.

Restless, edgy and needing Damon so badly it hurt, she tried to tell herself this was all the effects of whatever drug had been put in her drink and that Damon was only looking out for her by not touching her. But every wisp of air blowing in from an antiquated air conditioner tickled her skin like a lover wielding a teasing feather.

Her whereabouts were hazy. The passage of time even hazier. But her actual, physical senses were acute and she knew what was going on. Damon thought Nick Castine was following them. He'd carried her back into the club, back to some private hotel room available for customers of the place, so that he could avoid Castine.

Not for his benefit, she knew. But for hers.

Which was all well and good if Damon had at least put this bonus private time to good use. The room was a tacky, Gothic affair complete with red walls and silk sheets, which she now lay on, plagued by too much lust. But Damon hadn't touched her other than to feel her forehead and to keep her as cool as possible.

Didn't he know there was only one way to stop her from burning up inside? Wave after wave of unanswered hunger squeezed her womb, making it impossible to be still. Not even her most uptight impulses were enough to keep her from writhing around the bed like a cat in heat.

After the first hour and a half in the room with Damon, he had imported some doctor friend who was apparently a fellow Coastie. The guy—Tejal Desai, who didn't sound the least bit foreign with his Brooklyn accent—had taken her vitals and given her a cursory exam.

She understood she'd been given a drug and that Damon wanted to be sure she didn't succumb to any bad side effects, but the raging need in her blood was the side effect that felt the most dire.

That damn piece of lucky quartz crystal she'd been carrying around tonight sure hadn't done its job.

"I want to go home if you're not going to touch me," she announced, watching Damon's back as he spoke in hushed tones with the doctor who'd politely insisted she call him by his first name.

"You can ride with me," Tejal said to Damon, loud enough for her to hear. "I'm heading back to the San Juan Sector, so I can take you to her hotel. We can go out the back."

"We're going to wait for Enrique, Doc. I don't want to involve you any more than I have to. Enrique will give us a lift out of here and I'll pick up my car tomorrow."

Lacey twisted in the sheets, wishing they could jump in Tejal's car and leave. She wanted to be in her hotel room with Damon, seducing him into taking the edge off this horrendous drug that made her feel like a sex-crazed porn star in some low-budget flick.

"You think I've gone soft working in the medical office? I don't need you watching my ass, Craig." Tejal checked his timepiece. "How much longer before Enrique will be here?"

"He had to come from Borinquen." Damon frowned as he stared at Lacey on the bed. "But it shouldn't be much longer."

"Long enough for a quickie?" she asked, knowing she'd never say something like that in front of another man if it weren't for the drug running through her veins that seemed to shut down her filtering system.

Tejal coughed into his hand while Damon moved his friend farther away from her bed. Lacey had to strain to hear the rest of their conversation.

And no, she didn't much care that she was eavesdropping when it took all of her restraint just to keep a lid on her sexual urges.

The doc was speaking again, scrubbing a hand over a balding head that leaned more to the Ed Harris look than a cue ball.

"I'd stay if I thought she was in any danger, but her vitals are good and I don't think she ingested much of the drug. I'll test her blood back at the lab and let you know for sure, but she shouldn't suffer more than a hangover similar to a night of drinking." He shrugged. "We've seen plenty of Ecstasy cases at the clinic, and hyperthermia is the biggest cause for concern. Just make sure to keep track of her body temperature. If she starts to spike, bring her in and I'll open the urgent-care facility for you."

Lacey nearly wept with relief. The doctor was leaving. He'd practically said there wasn't a damn thing they could do for her at this point, so why did they need to hold back on giving her the, ah…medicine she needed most?

"Thanks, Doc." Damon took a thermometer from him and followed him to the door. "I know you don't make house calls—"

"House calls, no. But it's not the first time someone's called in a panic from this place." Tejal clapped Damon on the shoulder. "For that matter, we know when the deployable operations guys call in that there might be something bigger going down."

Damon nodded but remained silent as if he wasn't at liberty to talk about his work. Even through the drug-induced sensation, Lacey could tell Damon had more pull than she'd first realized.

"No need for comment," Tejal assured him, his Brooklyn accent sounding far too streetwise for an aging military doc. "And say what you will, I'm still going to sit out front until I see Enrique come in and exit safely with you."

He was half out the door before Lacey managed to call another thank-you, her brain starting to get wind of how much danger they might be in. Up until now she'd realized that Damon wanted to catch a big-time drug dealer. But she hadn't given much thought to the fact that the drug dealer was supposedly violent.

And that he might have had a hand in slipping Ecstasy into her drink.

As Damon closed the door on his friend, leaving them alone in this tacky, sex-drenched, pseudo hotel room, Lacey wasn't just faced with a man to whom she was wildly attracted; she now gazed at a man who would do anything to protect her. A man who just might hold her safety—her life—in his hands.

LACEY CAME AFTER HIM like a freight train.

Damon had barely shut the door behind Tejal and a boatload of worries about Lacey when she sprang out of bed and leaped into his arms, all warm woman and willingness.

She wrapped herself around him, her lips parting against his for a long moment until she dipped lower. Her tongue stroked upward along his neck and she repeated the motion over and over again on the same stretch of skin. He would have sworn the action must follow the path of some vein that led straight to his erection.

Talk about hitting below the belt.

"Lacey." He wanted to say more. To tell her what a bad idea this was, but she'd sort of stunned him. He stood there, holding on to her since she hadn't bothered leaving her feet on the floor, waiting for his brain to kick back into gear. "Enrique will be here soon. There are bad guys outside and we need to be ready to leave the minute we hear from him."

"I'm sorry I insisted on coming here." She pulled back, staring at him with blue eyes that weren't quite as dilated as they'd been earlier.

Thank God. Maybe she really was starting to shake off the effects of the drug someone had slipped into her drink. Tejal had taken her glass along with her blood sample so they'd know by dawn what had been used on her. Either way, Damon took it as a good sign that they seemed to have weathered the worst of her trip with no great ill effects other than discomfort on her part and a rage so thick he could barely swallow it on his.

"It's not your fault." He meant that. "I shouldn't have underestimated Castine. The sleazeball must have a reason for singling you out. He had to be behind this."

Damon knew that as sure as he stood here. He just didn't know what reason a drug kingpin would have for following around a Florida matchmaker on vacation in Puerto Rico, when the guy had a big deal ready to go down. The guy had taken a stupid risk that could screw up his whole operation. And while that might be great for Damon's mission, he couldn't allow anything to happen to Lacey in the process.

"I don't want to be responsible for you getting hurt." She murmured the words between kisses as she wrapped her legs tighter around his waist.

And, oh man, when was Enrique going to be here? Damon had been trained to stay focused under all kinds of distractions, most notably during the early stages of hypothermia or while battling the bends. But his training fell short when it came to maintaining reason with a hot woman intent on seduction stuck to him like a second skin.

"Believe me, I feel the same way about not wanting to see you hurt." Gently he pried her from him, unlocking her feet to set her back on the floor. He didn't think she'd slap him with a lawsuit for engaging in sex while she was still under the influence, but he had his own code of ethics to consider.

Touching Lacey right now wasn't a good idea.

His phone rang then, saving him from having to

justify his actions to her. Reminding him of the last cell-phone call he'd received…

God, it had been one hell of a night.

"Craig here."

"I'm inside, man." Enrique's voice had never been so welcome. "I'm looking at a tranny dressed like Barbara Streisand humping a stripper's pole, so please tell me we're getting out of here soon."

"You parked out front?" Damon peered around the crimson-colored back room that had been their hide-away for the last two hours and didn't see anything they'd left behind. He grabbed Lacey's hand and pulled her toward the door.

"Yeah. I gave the bouncer a deuce to make sure no one touches my car while it idles."

"We're coming at you from the west." Damon pushed his way through a crowd around the entrance to the handful of back rooms. Apparently, they were rented by the hour and had a quick turnover, making him regret that he'd had to bring Lacey into one of them at all. "I see you. Go back to the exit and we'll meet you there. I'll feel better if you're in the car before us."

"Can do."

Even from across the club, Damon could see Enrique part the crowd like Moses at the Red Sea. The guy was big and built like a Mack truck. He might have the good-ole-boy act down pat, but at the end of the day, no one messed with him.

Damon led them out a maze of narrow corridors that had to be fire hazards. He'd have to report the place for safety violations along with condoning the circulation of illegal drugs, but for tonight he was just grateful to get the hell out of there.

LACEY HAD NEVER BEEN so thankful to arrive in a hotel room.

A clean, gorgeously appointed hotel room where she didn't have to worry about drug dealers in Hummers coming after her or strangers slipping toxins into her drink.

The ride back to San Juan had been brief since Loiza wasn't far in miles, even though it felt like an abandoned little world all its own. Here, from the comfort of the El San Juan Hotel and Casino, she could look out at the water over Isla Verde, a stretch of shore comparable to Miami Beach for its glittering hotels and rampant tourism. Starbucks was here. Liveried doormen worked the entrances. Life felt safe again.

"How are you feeling?" Damon had come in ahead of her to check out the room. He'd searched for bad guys and wiretaps, listening devices and cameras before he'd allowed Enrique to escort her in.

"Fine." She pulled two waters from the minibar and tossed one to Damon. "Sort of good, actually. Like when you get a little buzz from wine, but I don't feel dizzy anymore."

Whatever she'd ingested now simply made her hyperaware of her body, her senses fine-tuned to the smallest detail.

In fact, right now she watched Damon move around the room with enviable speed, his mouthwatering body a tantalizing delight for her eager eyes. He double-checked the window, unplugged the phone and threw a spare blanket over the entertainment center where the TV perched alongside a series of photos of Isla Verde Beach.

"What are you doing?" she asked, ready to help in the hope she could still lure him into her arms tonight. Because even though the most intense edge of the drug had left her, she still felt itchy for him.

Her blood sang with need, her skin tight and tingly, as she waited and hoped that he would undress her and fix all that was wrong with her.

"Just making double sure there's no sign of anyone spying on you with cameras or other devices." He checked over the light fixtures beside the bed. Thankfully, his new task put him on the mattress, where she'd been waiting.

She lunged, tackling him where he sat. The surprise attack yielded delicious results and she sat on his chest a few seconds later, his heart pounding right below her spread legs. She thought she'd crawl right out of her skin if he didn't touch her soon. It seemed like she'd been suffering for hours. Days.

"I thought that's why we were going to turn the lights off." Grabbing the hem of her tank top, she tugged it up and off, launching it across the room to land on top of one lamp.

"Some cameras have night-vision technology." He flipped her over so fast she thought the wind was knocked out of her for a moment.

But no, that was just a side effect of the Ecstasy. He handled her carefully enough, she just felt everything to a higher degree. And, oh my, wouldn't that translate into a seriously hot time between the sheets?

"Damon, he doesn't even know I'm staying here."

She'd gotten the note from him back at her old hotel on the other side of the island. He had no reason to look for her in San Juan. "Besides, how good can the images be from a night-vision camera?"

She didn't want this hum of sexual energy to wear off before he touched her. After a whole life spent taking the more practical approach to men and sex—an approach inspired by her mother's blatant cow-eyed romantic perspective—Lacey liked how good it felt to not think about what she was doing. She was only concerned with how incredible Damon would make her feel.

"You might not appreciate even a blurry image of yourself posted on YouTube tomorrow morning."

Still, he moved to quickly finish whatever it was he was doing with the electronics in the room. Turning away from the lamp, he found her gaze and held it for a long moment before he turned off the light.

Darkness clouded the room, descending on her like a kinky blindfold. Her other senses leaped to life, channeling the unused visual stimulation into what she felt. Smelled. Heard.

A rustling a few feet away told her he'd moved closer. The swish of fabric sounded sort of like a shirt coming off as his steps padded near. Nearer.

She wrapped her arms around herself to still the trembling deep within her. In the dark she heard his breathing, steady but quick. Did he want this as much as she did?

The question rolled around in her head for a moment, reaching through the lust-fog to rattle her.

"Damon?" She stretched an arm out to find him while a shiver raced down her spine. "I want you. But I don't want you to, you know, do this just for me."

Although, with the way her body felt, she'd need to find some way to take the edge off or she'd never get any sleep tonight. It was already three in the morning.

"I won't do anything at all unless I'm sure you're out of the drug haze." His hands found her and guided her forward. "I wouldn't take advantage of you like that."

Two halting steps later she was plastered against his hard, lean length. His warm, broad chest. Muscular thighs. He'd left his T-shirt on, but gotten rid of the other shirt. His jeans did nothing to hide how much he wanted her.

Desire flooded her belly and breasts as a familiar tension knotted inside her.

Her fingers dug into his shoulders as her knees buckled from a fresh wave of hunger. "I don't think I can stand it if all we're going to do is cuddle."

A dark laugh ripped from his throat.

"Sweetheart, you may be the first woman in history to say that. But I'll bet there are other ways to take the edge off where I won't feel like I'm taking advantage." He toyed with the bra strap at her shoulder.

Her heart stuttered in her chest. "It's not like it would be the first time we touched each other, though. So how could you think it would be taking advantage of me?"

She had to try to appeal to his logic. Reason. Get around that damn stalwart sense of honor to convince him to be with her.

His hand worried the strap, making her crazy.

"Just because a woman says yes once doesn't mean she'll always say yes." He lowered his voice, the gravelly note sliding over her skin with a tingly caress.

"Maybe you don't recall, but our past sexual history

amounts to more than *once,* Damon Craig. And an honorable man would want to ease the worst of my symptoms and take care of me to the very best of his ability now that we're safe. Alone." She licked her lips, wanting to feel his kiss there.

"You sound pretty damn lucid to me," he growled, lowering his thumb into the satin cup of her bra. Hovering above the tight peak.

"Not at all like I'm in a drug haze, right?" She nipped his ear, so hungry for him she thought she'd go out of her ever-loving mind.

"I don't want you to regret this." He bit out the words through gritted teeth and she hated to think she was asking for more than he could give. But damn it, why couldn't he be reasonable?

"I'll regret going somewhere dangerous and drinking tainted soda, but I'm *not* going to regret asking for help getting through the night."

"How can I fight you?" His thumb finally descended to the taut peak of her aching nipple and circled.

The motion sent a ripple of excitement between her thighs, forcing her to grind her hips against him. The act was shameless. Wanton. And felt so damn good she wanted to cry.

"Please, please, please," she whispered, needing him so desperately she couldn't worry about the drugs in her system or what tomorrow might bring if a dealer was stalking her. Damon was here for her tonight and—finally—volunteering for duty.

He backed her away from the bed until her shoulder came upon something solid. The door to the bathroom maybe. Fleetingly, she wondered why he'd take her there, away from the comfort of expensive sheets and goose-down pillows, but mostly she wanted his hand inside her panties.

Sealing her lips to his, she stroked his tongue, drawing on it. With a wriggle of her hips and some help from her hands, she started to push down her skirt.

"Leave it," he ordered, breaking the kiss as he tugged her bra down to bare her breasts completely. "Leave it all on."

He lowered his mouth to a nipple, laving her with his tongue while his hands hauled up her skirt. Pushed aside her panties.

Pleasure exploded inside her even before he slipped his finger all the way in. Her release squeezed him hard, over and over again as wave after wave of fulfillment rocked her. He never let go of her, holding her steady against the door while her knees melted beneath her.

When the shudders slowed, he tipped back from her, as if to look at her even though they were still in total darkness.

"Are you okay?" He kept his hand between her legs, his palm hot and hard against her clit.

And sweet saints above, she wanted him all over again.

"Yes. Just—" She moistened her lips, unused to being so frank with a man. "I want you inside me."

"Your wish is my command." Releasing his intimate hold on her, he lifted her in his arms. "I'm taking us over to the bed, but I want you to pull the covers off and bring them with us to lie on the floor."

She tried to think about something besides the fire inside her, but her brain kept shutting down as if her sex drive had an override switch.

"Why?" she finally managed, snatching up the comforter when he swooped her down to the king-size bed.

"I can't fall asleep tonight while I'm watching over you." He carried her back toward the bathroom door—or somewhere away from the bed. She'd lost her bearings in the dark.

"Lay it down right here." He spoke close to her ear, his voice vibrating through her body since he held her close to his chest.

With an effort, she heaved the comforter to the floor and then wrapped her arms around his neck, more interested in getting him on top of her than worrying about blankets. She'd never been so uninhibited, so free to act on every naughty impulse, and she wouldn't waste a second of it.

So before they even made it down to the cotton ticking covering the floor, she reached between their bodies to stroke the hot, hard length of him.

Damon nearly stumbled to his knees at the unexpected feel of Lacey's hand caressing him. Only with superhuman concentration did he remain upright, gripping her tight in his arms as he lowered them both, carefully, to the floor.

Lacey might be lost in a world of sensation—some of which was probably still drug-enhanced—but he needed to remain alert. Sharp. He didn't trust that Castine hadn't followed them here, even though he hadn't seen any sign of a tail on Enrique's car.

But it sucked having to keep his wits about him when Lacey so obviously wanted him in every way humanly possible. The realization would have been even more tantalizing if she hadn't been wading through the last hours of an Ecstasy trip. As it stood, he needed to maintain a sense of her general heart rate and body temperature to be sure she didn't suffer any side effects. And he'd sure as hell be close enough to keep track of both those things. He'd drive her back to the base tomorrow for a follow-up, but for tonight, he couldn't let her suffer. Not when her eyes had cleared enough that he knew she understood what she was asking for.

Besides, he knew enough about the enhanced tactile responses in people who used Ex. He wouldn't subject her to sleeping in that big bed alone when she was so wound up she could hardly sit still.

This was for her benefit, damn it. Not for the good of his Johnson that was definitely loving every second of this.

"Lacey," he ground out between his teeth as her silky fingers smoothed a path down the thick vein running up his shaft. "I don't think you'll want to, ah, waste this time by not having me inside you."

Which was code for the fact he'd lose it any second if she kept this up. He rose to strip off his clothes before rejoining her.

"Really?" She sat up beside him, her hip bumping his knee as she made herself comfortable between his thighs. "I thought you might reward me all the more thoroughly if I paid more attention to you first." She circled the head with her fingertip and then bent forward until soft strands of her hair skimmed his hip. "Besides, every way we touch feels so good that I don't want to miss anything."

Her lips slid along the top of his shaft, a slick pressure that switched on a furnace inside him. The room was quiet except for the little sighs of pleasure she breathed against him, her mouth taking more and more of him until he thought he'd lose it.

Burying his fingers in her hair, he held her there for a long moment, wanting everything she offered him so sweetly. But he knew the drug would make her sexually restless and he planned to be inside her for as long as possible to take the edge off.

"Come here." He tugged her up by her shoulders, knowing damn well that one more caress of her nimble tongue and he'd be a goner. "You need this as much as I do."

He found her jaw and cupped it in one hand, guiding her close. He settled her on his lap, helping her straddle his thighs. She'd peeled off the rest of her clothes at some point, her curves exposed. As he aligned their bodies and a sweat broke out along his back from restraint, he wished like hell he could see her.

After he rolled on a condom, he stroked a thumb along her lower lip, feeling her expression even if he couldn't see it. She nipped the tip, drawing him into her mouth to suckle until he had no choice but to nudge his way inside her.

Her mouth went slack on his thumb and he could feel the way her head lolled back, her hair spilling lower on her shoulders as her neck curved. A low moan escaped her lips, vibrating through her whole body everywhere they touched.

Her skin felt hot and he knew a second's worry about side effects, but then he felt hotter than her. If either one of them was going to incinerate from this joining, it'd be him.

Plunging all the way inside her, he thrust deep. She

felt so good. The best. He'd never been with someone so willing to follow him anywhere—on the beach, against a tree, in strange hotel rooms—anytime.

And all at once he wanted it to be real. To be about more than helping her through an Ecstasy trip or keeping her away from Castine. He wanted this kind of all-consuming connection with someone when it wasn't attached to his job or her job or—

"It feels *sooo* amazing." Lacey wrapped her arms around him and kissed him, pressing every inch of herself against him as she ground her hips into his. "I don't think I'll ever get enough of this."

Her words touched him with a sincerity she couldn't possibly mean. And damn, but he couldn't let himself get caught up in a woman who would only be leaving at the end of the week. A woman who might very well be playing him.

Shoving aside the knot of contradictory thoughts, he lost himself in the heady glide of her body all around him. This much at least—this intense physical connection, the mind-blowing chemistry that had drawn him to her from the minute he'd laid eyes on her—that part *was* real. He couldn't deny it any more than he could pretend she wasn't getting under his skin in a big way.

Covering her mouth, he kissed her, savoring the way her whole body quivered at his touch. He stroked her tongue with slow, methodical sweeps and reached between their bodies to touch her clit in that same way, mirroring the caresses until she cried out. Tensed. Shuddered with another climax.

He let go then, relinquishing that tight restraint to let himself feel how good it was to be buried inside her. He followed her almost instantly, his blood roaring in his ears as he shouted her name. Clutched her to his chest like a drowning man would a life preserver.

The very thought humbled the hell out of him. Made him realize he might be over his head with her. With this investigation. With a life that had gone off the rails ever since his last girlfriend walked out.

But no matter how much he wanted some time and space to figure out what to do next, he wouldn't leave Lacey in the dark to fight off another wave of intense sexual hunger because of some drug *he* might have actually brought into her life. He'd been the one to intervene when she'd been on her ill-fated date with Castine. What if Damon's ties to the Coast Guard had brought all this attention to Lacey?

He would make damn sure tonight was the last time she suffered the consequences of knowing him.

9

LACEY SMILED as she opened her eyes late that morning. The night had been a blur, but it sure had ended on a high note.

Waking up on the floor of a decadent hotel room beside Damon, their clothes flung to the four corners like they'd been caught in a cyclone, she couldn't help smiling at what they'd shared.

Sitting up in the tangle of sheets they'd torn off the bed, she could see around her, thanks to the sunlight peeking through the sides of the window blinds. She remembered Damon leaving her side once more to take apart various light fixtures and air-duct vents to be sure the room was clean. He'd pronounced the place a hundred percent bug free before dawn.

"Morning." Damon stirred beside her, his eyes clear and alert even though he hadn't slept all night. "Are you feeling okay?"

She nodded, but the motion brought a small throb to her temple.

"For the most part." She massaged her forehead and tucked the sheet more tightly around her. She felt strangely domestic next to this man who was some kind of military supercop for illegal drugs. And a man like that shouldn't give her any warm fuzzies. "A little sore, maybe."

She'd noticed the burn between her legs when she sat up. Every muscle in her calves, thighs and glutes protested her movement.

He gave a short bark of laughter.

"Please tell me you remember instigating last night."

"I remember practically begging you to take off your clothes, yes." Grinning, she tucked a strand of hair behind her ear, self-conscious at being with him first thing in the morning when she must look like a train wreck. Visions of smeared makeup were already making her feel like a lowlife.

Damon, on the other hand, looked as hot as if he'd just stepped out of the shower. And maybe he had. His short hair hadn't moved an inch overnight.

But that wasn't all that appealed to her. Last night she'd seen a whole different side to him. A facet that was more than just fiercely protective. He'd been sensitive. Considerate to her needs. In many ways, he'd been the kind of man she would have chosen for herself based on her list of traits she would want in a man on her profiling system.

And knowing that—how close he came to what she wanted most—unsettled her in the bright light of the morning after. Especially when all of those wonderful traits were wrapped up in a tough-guy arrogance she normally would never go for.

"You tested my endurance to the limits, woman." He peered at her out of the corner of his eye before he got off the floor to put on his shorts.

Lacey's eyes followed him, amazed at the sharp definition of each muscle in his body as he moved. Admittedly, there were benefits to being with an unapologetic alpha male.

"But you have to remember it was for a good cause," she assured him. "I was suffering mightily before you agreed to help me."

"I'm called to serve." He roamed around the room, picking up his clothes, and she wondered if this morning felt as awkward for him as it did for her.

And wouldn't that be another lightbulb moment for her? Who said the alpha male had to feel secure in every situation? He only had to *behave* like he owned the world.

"So will your friend's medical lab give us scientific proof of what kind of drug I was given?" She remembered the enhanced sense of daring and the lowered inhibitions she'd felt, especially during the early part of the night. "Oh God."

She remembered something else, too.

"What?" He tossed her his T-shirt as he slid into his silk dress shirt.

"Did I practically hump you on the dance floor?" She recalled wrapping her leg around him in the club. While people were watching them.

"While I'd like to think you wanted to… No. You didn't." He retrieved his pants from an overstuffed sofa in the corner of the room.

"But I made a spectacle of myself nevertheless." She could recall all the sets of eyes on her and the way she'd flaunted herself shamelessly.

"It wasn't your fault." He slid into the pants and just like that, he also slipped into his lieutenant shoes, his cool, remote military side stepping into the room. "Es-

pecially since we think it was methylenedioxy-metham-
phetamine that went into your drink. Ecstasy is a psychedelic and a stimulant. Potent stuff."

Indignation flooded her all over again, especially
with Damon roaming around the hotel room like some
international spy, peering out the blinds at the beach
below and listening at the door as if the bad guys were
out in the hall about to bust in for a shoot-out.

Did he think someone had tracked them to the hotel
during the night?

"Tejal told me to come in and see him today." She
had no clue if her healthcare network would cover her
medical costs down here, but she'd pay out of pocket if
necessary. If there might be any long-term side effects
of this episode, she wanted to know.

"I'll go with you. If you don't mind driving us there,
I can find someone to take me out to Loiza and retrieve
my car." He peeled his gaze away from the parking lot
to gauge her response.

"Of course. I'd appreciate the help locating his office."

"Do you mind if I ask you about your friendship
with the woman you spoke to at the club last night?
Tatiana?" He took a seat on a chair close to the blankets
where she sat.

She pulled some of the covers up on her lap, needing
more of a barrier between them when she dealt with
Damon the military man. This wasn't the same person
who'd lavished attention on her for half the night,
feeding every one of her desperate, hungry needs.

"Sure." She reached for her bra under the bed and
wound it around her while keeping Damon's T-shirt in
place. She wasn't sure she could bare any more of

herself to him right now, not when the conversation had turned so tense.

"You said you met her at the beach."

"I bought a necklace from her at Playa del Vega Baja and she gave me a little good-luck stone for a present." She backed her arms out of the T-shirt sleeves and shoved them through the bra straps before redressing. "She struck me as sort of—"

"What?"

"Actually, she fit the whole counterculture stereotype, so maybe it's not surprising that she also sells drugs on the side." Her mother had never gone that far, but then, Lacey hadn't known her in the years of her wild youth.

Frustrated, she tossed aside the covers that she'd been hiding under and stalked around the room to hunt for clean underwear and a pair of shorts.

"Counterculture?" Damon picked up the blankets from the floor and laid them on the bed. "You mean like a flower child or something?"

"I guess. She had sort of this live-and-let-live vibe, and she kept talking about how beautiful Puerto Rico was." She burrowed in her suitcase on the other side of the bed which she hadn't bothered to unpack. "Come to think of it, I was sort of weirded out by some of the vials she had. They could have had drugs in them. I thought one looked like blood, but then I figured she must have been selling some kind of herbal stuff."

"Did you report her?"

"I hardly gave it any thought. She was showing off her wares on a public beach so I guess it didn't occur to me she'd really have something illegal among the leather anklets and shell necklaces." She dressed in khaki shorts and traded his T-shirt for a red one of her own. "Did I fail in my public duty?"

His gaze narrowed and she realized she'd gotten snippy. Uptight for very little reason. But then, according to her family, she did that a lot.

Before she could apologize, he rose from the chair and headed for the door.

"Not at all. You ready to go?" His jaw was set, and his cool, alpha-male face was very much in place again. Remote. Aloof. Captain America.

"Wait." She followed him to the door, recognizing her morning-after defensiveness. "I'm sorry. I don't have any right to give you a hard time when you're only trying to help me."

"You've been through a lot the past few days." Brushing a hand through her hair, he gave her an out even though she felt she didn't deserve one.

Her heart melted a little more. She fought the urge to lean into him. To lean *on* him. It would be all too easy to do with a man so capable and caring. No matter that she didn't know about his five- and ten-year goals or his top requirements in a romantic partner, she was falling for Damon Craig. And if she wasn't careful, she'd be in over her head before the week was out.

"And I'm ready to put it all behind me after we see the doctor." She kept her hands at her sides, unwilling to touch him when she was so vulnerable inside. "But I need ten minutes to hop in the shower first."

With a quick nod, he agreed to her terms while she hurried toward the bathroom. She reached the door when his cell phone rang. At the same moment, she realized she should bring some clean clothes with her and she detoured back toward her suitcase.

So it was completely by accident that she heard him answer the phone in his usual, clipped greeting.

"Craig here."

What surprised her as she searched for any pair of shorts that didn't need ironing was the way his voice changed dramatically the next moment.

"Kelly?" Damon's eyes flashed over to Lacey, his dark gaze uneasy.

Or was that her own insecurity talking?

Hurrying her pace, Lacey raced for the bathroom and shut the door behind her. She turned the hot water on full blast and let the sound of running water fill her ears. But even as the first drops hit the tile floor, she knew the pounding of the water would never drown out the memory of how Damon's voice had turned low and intimate for another woman. His tone had been secretive. Suggestive.

And as she stepped into the stinging spray of the hot jet stream, Lacey had to wonder if all that sensitivity she'd seen in him earlier had been in the imagination of a woman who still wanted to believe in the perfect match.

"YOU DIDN'T CALL ME BACK last night."

It took a moment for Kelly's words to penetrate his brain, since Damon's mind was on Lacey and what she must think of him taking phone calls from another woman while the sheets were still warm from their night together. He hadn't given much thought to what he was doing in an intensely physical relationship after a year of retreating from the dating world completely, but the awkward moment made him think about it now.

Because whether he and Lacey ever saw each other again after this week—an idea that rolled around in his head with enticing possibility—he had no business talking to Kelly now.

"I got tied up last night," he told her, all the while listening to the shower run in the next room. Where Lacey was currently naked and thinking he was a lowlife. He paced the floor to work off a mess of frustrations he couldn't fix right now.

"But I have information you need," she retorted, her voice sounding stronger and more emphatic than he remembered from their final conversations after their breakup, when she'd been tripping or strung out or both.

Had she cleaned up her act? Not that it mattered for a relationship that was dead and gone. But he hoped so for her sake.

"I'm listening." He felt more comfortable talking to her here than he had last night at the bar where anyone might overhear. Besides, he wasn't about to call her back from a landline if it meant he had to stay on the phone with her longer. He already felt like enough of a traitor to Lacey.

"I know you're at Borinquen now, and a few old friends of mine have been spending a lot of time partying down there the last few months."

"Is that right?" He tore his gaze from the bathroom door to key in to what Kelly was saying. No matter how he felt about her, if her connections as a user could help him bust Castine, he wouldn't hesitate to leverage them.

"Yes." She paused on the other end, then lowered her voice. "These girls have serious habits, and now that I've quit, I want to help them."

He wasn't going to ask about her addiction now, when he had to take Lace to the doctor. Better to focus on whatever information Kelly thought she had. Back when he'd known her, she'd been sharp. She'd taken pride in her logical approach to life. If she was clean again, she might have some great insights to offer on Castine's business. But if not…he had to suspect her motives.

"And how do you think you're going to do that?"

"By telling you what I've heard about their supplier. He's a big gun, Damon, and I know that's who your group goes after whether you admit it or not."

"C'mon, Kel. Not on the phone, okay?" He knew a moment's regret about not having a more secure connection, but damn it, she'd known him long enough to understand she shouldn't talk about his work on the phone.

"Right. Anyway, this guy is hosting a party barge that leaves out of Rincon."

Damon tensed, recognizing the name of the nearby beach community famous for its big waves and surfing. This was the same event Castine had told Lacey about.

"Are you sure?"

Rincon was damn close to the Coast Guard Air Station at Borinquen. Castine would have to be pretty damn cocky to think he could pull off something so blatant right under the Coast Guard's nose.

"Supersure. They invited me down for the launch party, but I'm staying out of that circuit." She hesitated. "I messed up by getting involved with it in the first place."

The soft, confidential tone sounded like a woman who wanted to segue into true-confessions time. Or maybe revisit old-relationship ground. And that damn well wasn't happening.

"Kelly, I need names. People names. Ship names. Do you have anything more concrete for me?"

"No. But I hear the ringleader is going to be on board this barge. My friends can't wait to meet him because he's supposed to be supergenerous to the women he, um, likes best."

"Nice friends you've got there, Kel." He shook his head as the water stopped running in the next room and he wondered how he'd ended up with a woman whose values were so far removed from his own. "Thanks for the tip."

"Damon?" Kelly sounded worried all of a sudden. "I'm really sorry."

She didn't clarify what she was sorry for. The drugs? Trolling for a new guy behind his back? But then, he didn't need to know. He was sorry for a few things himself. He might not have cheated on her with another woman, but he'd placed her second for their whole relationship.

"Me, too." As he stared at the bathroom door again, imagining Lacey wrapping her warm, wet body in a towel, he recalled exactly why he shouldn't try and see her after this week was over.

Thumbing the off button to disconnect, he swallowed the old regrets easier than the newest one. He wouldn't be able to discuss Kelly's phone call with Lacey any more than he could discuss any of the specifics of the upcoming operation to corner Castine with his newest shipment.

Ignoring the pang of conscience that told him there ought to be a better way, he phoned Enrique to relay the newest information. Once again he put his work first. Nothing had changed except that this new woman in his life was a hell of a lot tougher to relegate to the back burner than his ex had been.

Damon didn't know what aspect of that realization sucked worst. The discovery that maybe he hadn't cared about Kelly as much as he'd once thought? Or the news that Lacey Sutherland already meant more to him than any woman he'd ever known?

"Is it just me, or does it seem like two people who've boinked as much as we have ought to know each other better than we do?"

Lacey's words were so unexpected later that morning that Damon had to laugh.

His thoughts had been a million miles away for most of their drive out to Borinquen. He'd convinced her to let another military doc look her over, since Tejal had been called out on duty somewhere for the day. The urgent-care facility in San Juan was crowded and the wait time would have been long anyhow. Plus, he needed a way to get to work without his car since they'd left it at In the Flesh.

Now, cruising west on Route 2 toward the base, they drove past 1001 small shops selling car parts that seemed to thrive in this section of the island. Wind whipped over them with the top down, the warmth of another perfect day at odds with the formerly somber mood in the car.

"Boinked?" He drummed his fingers on the steering wheel as he swerved around a pothole.

"You have to admit, things got hot and heavy so quick that we haven't really talked about regular stuff," she explained, glancing at him across the console, her blond hair all the kinkier after her quick shower before they left her hotel room.

In her red T-shirt with no makeup and her natural curls flying, she looked like a surfer chick right down to the freckles dotting her nose. He hadn't noticed those before and guessed they were something the days in the sun had brought out.

"Maybe you have a point." He was just glad she hadn't brought up the phone call that he couldn't discuss. At least not until Castine was in custody. "Are you planning to use those matchmaking skills to figure out why we're so hot together?"

He wove the rental around an iguana sunning himself on the road. As they neared a local beach, the smoky scents of barbecued meats wafted through the vehicle.

"Don't you want to know how our profiles sync up?" He heard the challenge in her voice. There was something endlessly prickly about this woman. Starchy, almost.

Oh, it hadn't been there last night. Sex in general seemed to make it disappear. But she had a natural defensiveness about her whether they were talking about her job or her personal life. Curiosity about her— about what made her that way—prompted him to realize she might be onto a good idea after all.

There could be some value in learning more about the people you got close to. If he'd thought to get to know Kelly on a deeper level, maybe he would have understood how vulnerable she'd been, left on her own in the middle of Nowheresville, Alaska.

But while it might be interesting to see what made Lacey tick, what the hell might she read into him if he filled out that damn profile she put so much stock in?

"I guess," he hedged, feeling off his game today. And

thank God the medical center wasn't too much farther. "But I've got my hands full this afternoon."

He needed to follow up on the lead Kelly had given him about the party barge out of Rincon and pin down the origins of the drug Lacey had been given last night.

"Oh. We don't have to analyze the profiles today anyhow. I'm not feeling my best, to be honest." She tilted her head sideways onto the fist she'd propped up with an elbow on the door.

Her admission sucker punched him, reminding him he needed to treat her with a little more sensitivity while her body still processed the aftereffects of the drug. No doubt the chemical wouldn't be out of her system for another ten or twelve hours.

"We're almost to the medical center." He sped up to pass an old junker painted with political messages and advertisements. "The docs there will take better care of you than I have."

She was quiet for so long he turned to look at her and saw her smiling.

"Don't sell yourself short. You took damn good care of me last night."

And just like that, they were connected again somehow, held together by fragile, invisible links that wouldn't disappear just because he thought it was for the best. He was attracted to Lacey Sutherland, and no matter how much he buried his head in the demands of his job, that wasn't going to change anytime soon.

He just hoped he could distance himself from that attraction enough to let her leave at the end of the week without any regrets.

"So," Lacey began, tugging a strand of curls off her

cheek as they stopped at the last traffic light before the base. "Even if we don't analyze them, we could at least start the process by filling out the matchmaking profiles when we have extra time. I have one in my purse if you're going to be bored in the waiting room."

Aw, crap.

He was cornered, but he couldn't renege now. Not when he owed her some compassion for what she'd been through. For that matter, he owed her job more respect than he'd given it in the past. But it looked as if that distance he'd wanted wasn't going to happen anytime soon.

HE NEEDED TO GIVE UP on Lacey.

Nick's rational mind recognized this. Understood it. Agreed with it.

Too bad he'd passed the point of no return with her.

He used one of his aliases to check into the El San Juan Hotel and Casino, the same hotel where she was staying. He'd had her followed last night after she and her boyfriend had eluded him. Nick had already snuffed the guy in charge of that operation. What idiot left a calling card like two big-ass Hummers? That was fine if you wanted to make a statement. Intimidate someone. But that's not the way a serious operator went about getting real business accomplished. If the douche bag had waited for Lacey and her boyfriend in a beat-up old Toyota the night before, Nick would have already sampled her flesh. Introduced her to exotic pleasures G.I. Joe had probably never even heard of, let alone tried.

Now, too many people in his organization knew that he wanted her. That he'd failed more than once to complete the mission. And that just wouldn't do.

Drug runners were a breed apart. A group made up of big balls and even bigger egos. If Nick's men thought he didn't have the *cojones* to pull off his chosen missions, they'd align themselves with some brash young upstart who did.

Still, their concerns would all be put to rest when they learned his bigger plan for her. Then they'd see she hadn't been just a plaything for the boss. Getting close to her would be seen as a strategic move for the operation.

"Here you are, Mr. Cassidy." The hotel attendant smiled as she handed him the key card to his room. "Just take the elevators to the fourth floor and we hope you'll enjoy your stay."

"Is it possible to obtain a map of the hotel?" he asked, not sure if he would need it, but wishing to be prepared for all possible scenarios.

The Coast Guard man was a nuisance he was well rid of. Damon Craig had proven troublesome to the larger operation as well as to Nick's personal venture with Lacey. Thankfully, he'd secured the outside help of the man's druggie ex-girlfriend to ensure Craig would be chasing his tail for a while.

"Of course." The woman leaned forward on the counter to present the map to him, her ample breasts stretching the fabric of her blouse in a way that would draw any man's eye.

She had no idea what she was getting herself into with him. But how could he resist a small snack to tide himself over until he could secure the elusive meal he'd been hungering for all week?

"Thank you." He tucked the map into his jacket pocket and smoothed his tie. "And would it be too forward of me to ask you for a tour at some point? In exchange for dinner, perhaps?"

The young woman's cheeks flushed pink as she bit her lip.

"We do try to keep the guests happy," she admitted, tucking a dark curl behind her ear as she jotted down her digits with the other hand and passed him the card. "Just let me know when you'd like me to play tour guide."

His body responded predictably to the invitation, although not as much as it might have if the failure with Lacey didn't still weigh on his ego. No doubt the curvy desk clerk would pay for that loss until Lacey was brought to heel.

All in good time.

"I'll look forward to it," he assured her, slipping the card in his pocket right next to the home address of his other future bed partner.

Because Nick would have Lacey sooner or later, even if he had to follow her all the way back home for a block of uninterrupted time with her. When Lacey was finally in his bed, he would indulge his every last desire.

10

"'YOU'VE JUST PURCHASED the newest, most technologically advanced camera on the market. Do you read the directions or simply begin using it?'

"What the hell kinds of questions are these?" Damon muttered to himself as he read the twentieth query in Lacey's compatibility questionnaire. He sat in the waiting room outside the infirmary, feeling restless that he wasn't in the office yet and guilty that he hadn't brought Lacey directly here the night before.

What if she'd been slipped a stronger drug than Tejal suspected?

Damon's pencil hovered over his answer—who read directions when they got a new gadget to mess around with?—when his cell phone rang. Stepping out into the hall with Lacey's test under one arm, he thumbed the on button and saw from the ID it was Enrique on the other end.

He'd already set the wheels in motion to follow up on the lead from Kelly.

"Craig here."

Medical personnel brushed by him while the facility's PA system paged a doctor. He stepped into an old phone booth and used the empty seat behind the small screen for privacy.

"Where are you, bro? We've got reports of major activity coming up from the south."

He tensed, knowing he needed to quit overthinking the dating profile and get his ass in to work.

"Have we run flights to confirm it?" They'd been waiting for a day of unusual watercraft activity as a potential sign of Castine on the move. In the past he'd flooded this section of the Atlantic with a variety of small, private vessels as a decoy from his boats' movements.

"We're checking out some bigger vessels farther out to sea along with any barge headed toward Rincon. Our intel is suggesting the latest shipment is too big to hide in a handful of smaller boats." Enrique's voice picked up volume as the background noise increased and Damon recognized the sounds of the flight line nearby.

He'd thought he had a personal reason to intercept drugs on the move before, when he'd been full of resentment about Kelly's descent into addiction. But now the illicit crap floated freely around every major U.S. city to the point where it had ended up in Lacey's drink without her knowing.

He would find out who wanted to hurt her. And if it was Castine, the way his gut had been telling him, he would crush the bastard and his whole operation.

"I'll be there as soon as I can." He didn't have any flight time scheduled for the day, but that didn't mean he couldn't be on base, ready to go if their intel guys turned up something. Pocketing his phone, he decided to check in with Lacey and go. He'd fix this problem at the root, and that meant putting duty before playing Joe Chivalry here.

He didn't need to read the manual to know it was time to make tracks.

"HE ABANDONED YOU in some foreign hospital *alone* while you suffered from a drug trip?" As Lacey sat by the hotel pool later that morning, her sister screeched in her ear through her cell phone from a few thousand miles away.

Lacey had wanted her sister to know about her doctor's visit even though she'd been avoiding Laura ever since their competition had heated up. No matter how much they picked at each other professionally, they remained close on a personal level.

A gifted child, Laura had finished college before most of her friends had declared a major. But speeding ahead of the world with her brilliant mind had never made her socially aware. She could rub people the wrong way with her manner, but she basically meant well. Lacey had been annoyed when her mathematician sis decided to follow her into the matchmaking business, but she was now beginning to believe that Laura simply couldn't bear to watch other people doing things that she could accomplish in a smarter, faster, better way.

"The drug trip was over by then," Lacey assured her, exhausted from a night of so little rest. "And it's not a foreign hospital, since Puerto Rico is a U.S. territory. I was in very good hands."

And how. She'd be thinking about Damon Craig's hands for a long time. Too bad that memory had been tainted just a little by the mystery phone call from an unknown woman afterward. Although she hadn't read Damon's profile yet, she didn't believe he would date another woman at the same time as her, so she wasn't worried about that.

But what if he harbored feelings for someone else that he hadn't acted on?

"So you called to make sure I knew that the family good girl had her first drug trip, but basically you're fine?" Laura sounded less worried and more perturbed now.

How was it her sister could cut down her motives to nothing in two seconds flat?

"No." Damn it. She *did* have a valid reason for calling. "I thought it would be wise for a family member to be aware of a health issue in case I have any delayed effects from the experience. You're listed as my emergency contact for medical purposes, you know."

"Ah. Ever the organized and practical." Laura must have been sitting on her porch because Lacey could hear the multitude of wind chimes in the background. Her home was a temple to all things hippie. "So how's the blog going?"

Lacey was grateful for the lack of people around the hotel's exotic pool near the beach. She'd commandeered a private cabana in a back corner that didn't have true walls or a ceiling but silky curtains surrounding it that allowed her to see anyone else approach. The content of her blog—her experiences at In the Flesh—was material that she couldn't speak openly about in public without a bit of discomfort.

Funny that talking about her matchmaking business could be as socially awkward as discussing a drug trip.

"I'm going through a professional crisis, but other than that, just fine."

"Please don't say you're still hung up on the number of visitors." Laura hushed her poodle, Brillo, when the dog started to yap like crazy. "I told you the ebbs and flows of those trends mean nothing in the big mathematical scheme of things. If you took ten minutes to check out a statistics textbook, you'd see they're in keeping with the laws of probability."

Lacey would have a headache after three minutes of a statistics textbook, so that wasn't going to happen. She wondered how her kooky, astrology-loving sister had ended up with such a mathematically inclined brain. No surprise her twin had never really put her degree to use. But then, maybe Laura had just been in a hurry to get to college to study most anything in order to get out of their house, the same way Lacey had been. And wasn't that an epiphany for the day? Maybe Laura hadn't come through their shared childhood as unscathed as Lacey had always imagined.

"Even if you're right about that, advertisers don't care about some theories an old Roman spouted about math. They look at visitor numbers." Lacey had overhauled her whole matchmaking system, and still wasn't confident she'd yield any better results when she uploaded it next week. Her obsessive online checking from the queen-size lounger at poolside told her there hadn't been any significant jump in the site's users or her blog's readers, but maybe her newest entry would cause more of a stir.

She'd learned a few things about human nature last night at In the Flesh that might change her whole dating outlook. First of all, she couldn't trust people's knee-jerk response that they *weren't* looking for love or lasting intimacy; even those who said they weren't ready to commit had admitted—upon deeper questioning—

that they would be open to a lasting relationship with the right person.

That new knowledge proved that people didn't always know what they were looking for until they found it. Something Damon had effectively expressed to her from the night they met.

"Sure, they look at numbers. Just not very well." Laura turned up some Native American wind flute music as if to drown out her dog with the instrument. "My system's strengths are that I offer a comprehensive personality inventory and spin the stats in every way imaginable. That's fun for people but I don't ever suggest the data means a whole hell of a lot."

"Yes, but they can read most anything they want into your stats since you don't interpret them. They've got a fifty percent chance of this, a thirty percent chance of that—"

"Because matchmaking is like meteorology to me. All I can do is make some predictions and entertain on the way."

Lacey sighed. "And you with a science-based degree. Doesn't something seem wrong about that?"

"Attraction isn't a science."

Where had she heard all this before? "Spoken like a woman whose Web site isn't in peril." Lacey clicked through the hits to the Connections site and saw that some of the visitors had come from other dating Web sites, which was typical.

A few, however, came from more risqué sites. Naked-chick Web pages. Web sites promoting sex-enhancement products.

Normal enough. But the percent of hits from those places seemed high.

"You know, Lacey, sometimes confronting your worst fear removes a great deal of stress from life."

"Are you suggesting I should lose my business on purpose?" Maybe her sister had been inhaling too much incense. "How about I just get a wind flute CD and crank up the music a little louder instead?"

"At least I won't be combating ulcers by the time I'm forty."

Lacey paused to consider that, wondering if Laura had a point. The stress had been eating her up lately. The doctor this morning—who hadn't been nearly as cute as Tejal—had asked her about her blood pressure and sleep habits, finding both of them sub par.

Maybe she was working too hard.

"Then I guess I'll get back to my vacation so I can keep my toes in the sand and my mind off work."

"While you're dodging drug runners and a puddle pirate who is too busy saving the world to look out for you? Good luck with that."

Lacey had the urge to stick her fingers in her ears and shout over top of her sister's words, an ancient ploy that had never worked well since Laura's hippie bent—present from her earliest years—had given her a ridiculous amount of patience.

"Thank you," Lacey told her, taking the high road.

"I'm not even kidding, sis. You'd better be careful down there."

They disconnected, and Lacey tried to close her laptop and soak up the sun. But she couldn't quite conquer the need to keep a finger between the keypad and the monitor, holding her place as if she was in the middle of *War and Peace.* Just in case she needed to revisit her compatibility charts for people with extrovert tendencies.

Who could relax like that? Answer—no one. Subtext of that answer—Lacey never relaxed. She thought about work all the time.

Or she had until this week when there had been some notable hours in which work had been the furthest thing from her mind.

Maybe she didn't need to relax in the sun as much as she needed a certain lieutenant.

The idea rocked her. She'd never *needed* a man. Her mom's dependency on guys had taught her how destructive the pattern could be. But maybe instead of growing into the independent woman she'd wanted to be, she'd merely traded one dependency for another.

Because Lacey *needed* her work. There were no two ways about it. She could practically feel the ulcer coming on already.

So, rather than give her sister the satisfaction of being right, she reached for her phone to call the only man who'd ever been capable of capturing her attention so thoroughly she wouldn't think about her job.

Clearly Damon Craig was therapeutic for her. And as long as she was only indulging in her chosen therapy during vacation, there was no risk of turning into her mother—convinced each new man she dated could save her from the train wreck of her life.

As his phone rang on the other end, she closed her laptop all the way and allowed herself to anticipate hearing his voice.

"I NEED YOU to take the first flight back home." Damon didn't mince words when Lacey called.

He'd been planning to get in touch with her himself after the afternoon briefing. He'd followed up on the lead from his ex, and the information had proven solid. The Coast Guard had located several possible barges that could be headed toward Rincon, two of which had known connections to Castine's operation. The lead had been well timed. Critical.

So critical it smelled like a setup to him. He'd argued against the quick movement of deployable resources to the waters off Rincon, but with no concrete reason to disbelieve the new information, he hadn't convinced his CO to wait. But Damon's every sixth sense was tingling, urging him to get Lacey out of town before Castine put his plans into motion.

"Excuse me?" She sounded like a miffed English teacher waiting for him to say "may I" instead of "can I." Something about her voice made him smile inside despite all hell breaking loose around them.

"Sorry. That was a crap excuse for a greeting, I know." He shoved a few files into his desk and walked out of his office for privacy. "What I mean is—the shit is hitting the fan around here. Castine's buddies have been all over the island in the past twenty-four hours. The activity means he's close to making a move."

He wasn't telling her anything he shouldn't. Half of Puerto Rico knew about Castine's reputation and that he was a person of interest to the Coast Guard.

"I don't understand." Her voice broke up, the cell-phone connection weak. "How does that affect me? If

Castine is busy with his business interests, won't he be less apt to bother me?"

"We haven't ruled out that he doesn't see you as a business interest." He couldn't speak at liberty here, on an unsecured phone. But he wanted to see her. Needed to get her on a plane headed home.

No matter that he'd been more attracted to her than he could remember being with any other woman. She'd made it clear she only wanted the kind of relationship he couldn't give right now—his first priority had to be the commitment he'd made to his job. He'd been a military man long enough to know relationships had a high mortality rate around here. Especially for guys like him who didn't leave anything on the field.

Or, in his case, in the air.

"What is that supposed to mean? I haven't been ruled out as a business interest?" Her voice had picked up a healthy dose of irritation. "Do you really think I'm down here to buy myself a caseload of club drugs?"

"No." He shouldn't have started this conversation here. Not when Lacey didn't have a clue about the information he'd learned today. "We need to meet as soon as possible. I can leave right away."

He would ask her to come here, but he had to pick up his car, and besides, she was already close to the airport in San Juan. He just wanted to see her long enough to convince her that leaving was for the best.

In fact, when she heard what he had to say, she'd probably sprint for the nearest aircraft of her own free will. And as much as he knew that's what had to happen, the vision of her leaving had already drained something out of him. A piece of him that he was going to miss.

"I can meet you by the hotel pool or down in the casino." She sniffed on the other end, and he figured she must be unhappy with him to downgrade him from sharing her bed to meeting in public places.

"The casino is fine. But stay indoors in public places where people can see you at all times." He checked his watch as he walked past a row of trees heavy with orange flowers toward the parking lot and Enrique's truck. "I'll be there in two hours."

He was half-dead on his feet from no sleep the night before and the long drives back and forth between the west coast of the island and San Juan, but he'd crash in the pickup. He'd been awake this long floating in the Atlantic during his training days, so he could damn well manage a little exhaustion on dry land.

"Fine." Was it his imagination or did she sound disappointed? "Did Tejal or one of the other doctors ever get back to you about the blood they drew from me?"

"No one phoned you?" He spotted Enrique jogging toward him, keys in hand. "They were supposed to speak to you directly, but they did confirm it was Ecstasy."

Guilt nagged him for a whole lot of reasons when it came to her and this was just one more. Unfortunately, the docs based in Borinquen hadn't seen Lacey as relevant to the drug runners the Coast Guard had been chasing and had no doubt dropped the ball in taking care of her, if they hadn't informed her of the confirmed substance.

"Great. I'll contemplate my sordid history as a user while I wait for you."

Damon slid into the truck as Enrique unlocked it. He thought how he was going to miss her sense of humor along with a whole lot of other things when she left.

Clicking off the connection, he leaned his head back in the seat as Enrique took the wheel. Normally Damon hated riding shotgun, but right now he didn't mind so much.

It would give him time to figure out how in hell he was going to say goodbye to Lacey so he could go after Castine full throttle.

THE STARBUCKS near the lobby was in full view of the casino, so Lacey figured she may as well spend her money on a grande caramel macchiato as opposed to the slot machines. She clutched her drink in her hand, savoring the warmth and the intoxicating java scent as she settled into one of the overstuffed couches near the lobby to wait for Damon.

So he could convince her to leave town.

And wasn't that the way of it with her and men? She didn't normally give them the time of day—too busy, too choosy—but when she did, they didn't want to be anywhere near her. Of course Damon wanted to boot her back to the States now that she'd uncovered intriguing new facets of him that attracted her brain as much as her body. Judging by how disappointed she'd felt on the phone today, she'd have to guess her heart had gotten involved in the mix, too.

The lobby of the El San Juan was a far cry from where she'd been last night. The rich mahogany moldings were thick and elaborately carved, trimming doors and walls with extravagant details. The sitting area where she'd retreated with her coffee boasted big carved wooden pillars that separated the space into intimate, smaller conversation nooks. Each of the four enclaves featured a small dome in the ceiling, furthering the sense that she'd stepped into a high-brow personal living room instead of a busy public space. It helped that no one else had chosen to join her in the sitting room closest to Starbucks.

From her vantage point, she watched the roulette wheel, wondering where Damon would head in a casino. Would he like the mathematical appeal of blackjack the way her sister did? The James Bond sexiness of baccarat? Or the simple ease of the slots?

"Lacey." His voice behind her startled and soothed her at the same time. In the few days that she'd known him, she'd formed a sharp, automatic response to simply hearing him speak.

Turning, she found him clutching his own coffee—generic black brew in a plain paper cup he must have bought on the way. He looked dark and dangerous with his unshaven face and the hollows under his eyes.

"You should be in bed," she informed him, gesturing to the seat beside her. "You're exhausted."

"I'm fine." He settled beside her, checking out the people around them as if he wanted to be sure she'd chosen well. "How are you feeling?"

He scrutinized her with eyes that missed nothing, taking in every detail of the slinky green dress she'd bought at the gift shop, the tiny spaghetti straps and surplice cut sexier than her usual fare. It wasn't often she wanted to turn heads, but she'd like to think tonight she would fare better than normal in that department. Her heels alone—purple crushed-velvet sandals with a square-cut green stone at the toes—could catapult any woman from so-so to sultry.

"I feel much better than last night." Sipping her

coffee, she savored Damon's eyes on her as much as the sweet blend of caramel syrup and caffeine. "Tejal was right—no hangover feelings. And I called the second doctor tonight to follow up on the news that I'd taken Ecstasy. He assured me there was no reason to worry about delayed effects."

She'd weathered her first drug trip with flying colors. Too bad she couldn't say the same about her first vacation fling. Not only was she falling for Damon Craig hard and fast—she was doing it with such little success that he couldn't wait to boot her out of town.

"Good." He drained the last of his coffee and rose to toss the cup. "Why don't we walk around for a minute?"

He had that steely, superspy look about him, the one that reminded her he was as married to his job as she was to hers. She had no idea why he wanted to take a stroll around the hotel now of all times, but she didn't mind.

"Okay." Still holding her coffee in one hand, she slid her other arm through his, and it occurred to her he'd already changed out of his uniform. "Did you retrieve your car from Loiza today?"

He steered them around the fringes of a bar where long, thin strips of glass and mirrors were suspended from the ceiling. A wind chime to end all wind chimes if a breeze ever blew through the bar.

"Yeah. No signs of any Hummers. I had a few cigarettes stubbed out on the hood, but otherwise, everything was fine. Our intel office contacted the police and confirmed the vehicles are owned by Castine's importing business. In particular, one is the company car for a higher-up who was reported missing by his wife this afternoon."

"Was that what you wanted to tell me over the

phone?" She'd been curious about the urgency behind his need to see her—and his desire to send her home. "What do you think that means?"

"I'm not at liberty to speculate on that. And no, that's not what I needed to tell you." His jaw flexed, his body tense as he brought her into the casino and leaned close to whisper in her ear. "I did a little outside research of my own today and discovered Castine might be using matchmaking Web sites to meet women. As a sex addict, he might have resorted to new means to fulfill the need."

"Excuse me?" Her coffee sloshed over the rim of the sipping slot as she came to a halt.

"Let's keep moving, okay?" Damon peered around the place and it occurred to her maybe he thought someone was following him. Them. "I don't have confirmation on the addiction diagnosis. It's a slippery label by clinical psychological standards and hasn't really been investigated by our people, because up until now it hasn't been relevant to the main charges we hope to lodge against him."

Lacey blinked, trying to process too much at once. She let Damon lead her past the slot machines, where an old Puerto Rican woman in a glittery blue pantsuit pumped quarters into a machine. The woman winked at Damon before going back to her quarters.

"Why is it relevant now? Because he suggested I check out a sex club?" She kept her voice low, but she wanted answers. The pieces he'd offered didn't fit together.

How could he have possibly used her matchmaking site to meet her?

"He might have started selling club drugs because he's a user himself. If he's meeting as many women as we believe, he may be plying them with drugs to coerce them into having sex with him. And if he's guilty of those kinds of crimes, it would be imprudent to haul him in until local police have the evidence they need for their own prosecution process."

Lacey watched the woman in the pantsuit play and wished she could be so serene. So oblivious to the dark undercurrents that swirled around her.

"Won't drug trafficking put him away long enough for everyone to be happy?"

"That's not fair to his victims who want to see him tried for crimes against them. Apparently he's been rumored to be behind a night of debauchery at that club in Loiza before where four different women say someone gave them Special K—Ketamine—and raped them in a back room before releasing them."

Lacey recognized the name. The so-called date-rape drug gave victims amnesialike symptoms, similar to if they'd been given anesthesia. She shuddered, wondering if she'd come close to that kind of experience.

Damon steered her away from the slots to a back corner by the VIP rooms.

"Are you allowed to tell me why you think he's using matchmaking sites to meet women?" She couldn't imagine Damon meant *her* site was involved.

Clients at Connections didn't pick one another's profiles the same way they might at other, simplified sites that let members mingle in a glorified cyber bar scene. Connections couples only met because they were chosen to meet. They had compatibility on numerous levels.

"I can't tell you why." He slung his arm around her as another couple emerged from one of the VIP rooms.

The weight of Damon's arm around her back drew her closer to his side, creating an intimate place to talk even amid the crowd, the blinking lights and endlessly ringing machines.

"Connections uses excellent security—" She broke off, recalling the odd influx of cyber visitors from illicit sites. Could someone have breached the site security while her focus had been elsewhere? Had she been so preoccupied with the ninety-six-percent compatibility stat and figuring out why her system had failed that she'd missed one of the most obvious answers in the book?

It wasn't her system.

It was a virus or some other form of cyber sabotage.

"What?" Damon squeezed her at the waist, as if he could spur a response.

"That security was excellent six months ago, but I guess that doesn't mean it's still good now. For that matter, I noticed some glitches in our site this morning. Do you know what this means if someone compromised the Connections Web site?"

"It means you were coerced into meeting this guy, and you need to get out of the line of fire before he comes after you again." Damon's eyes were so dark, so wickedly intent that she almost felt sorry for any bad guy he'd ever faced.

"Well, my first thought is that maybe the profiling system didn't fail. Maybe the system was corrupted through tampering and my match with a criminal wasn't the system's fault at all." The possibility shimmered before her like a mirage, a perfect, logical answer that needed confirmation but would be the answer to a whole lot of professional problems.

"My God, I can't believe you." Damon released her waist, only to take her by the hand and pull her toward the exit.

"Where are we going?" She tossed her coffee cup in a trash can as she struggled to keep up.

He didn't even bother looking back at her as he led her through the lobby toward the elevators.

"I'm going to talk sense into you while I help you pack."

11

"THIS IS A HELL OF A TIME to check your e-mail, Lacey."
Damon had pulled her suitcase out the moment they
entered her hotel room, but she'd sprinted toward her
laptop as if her life depended on it.

"I need answers about the security of our program.
Do you realize I've been having a complete career
meltdown over the false match my system gave me and
the declining satisfaction surveys? I need to check—not
just for my own peace of mind but to safeguard my
clients." Her fingers hammered the keyboard, flying
over the letters as she typed.

"You can do that on the plane." Damon nudged the
suitcase closer to where she sat on the bed, laptop in hand.

She looked sexy as hell in her hot dress and crazy
purple shoes. He even liked the little wire-rimmed
glasses she'd slid onto her nose when she'd sat down,
the lenses exaggerating the size of her eyes. Her whole
get-up was a far cry from the clubbing clothes she'd
worn last night and he wondered how many faces this
woman had. Would he have uncovered more sides to her
if he could have gotten to know her better? Longer?
There was something chameleonlike about her personality, as though she enjoyed fitting in more than standing

out. Although, now that he thought about it, the purple shoes weren't exactly ordinary. She put a Lacey stamp on things, even if she tailored herself to suit the moment.

"Damon." She paused her manic typing. "My flight doesn't leave until Sunday. Do you really think it's necessary I run all the way home to Florida to avoid one man?" She gave him the over-the-glasses librarian glance. "It's not like a whole army is searching for me. Or a gang."

"Did you hear the things I said about this guy?" He grabbed her bathing suit off the back of a nearby chair and tossed it on her suitcase, ready for her to pack.

"Yes, I did. And I will change hotels again if you think it's necessary, but I didn't just come here for the hell of it, Damon. I'm having some kind of—I don't know. Life reevaluation. And something about the sun and the relaxed attitude here is helping me heal some old insecurities." She flipped the laptop screen to face him. "And I just received word that the blog I posted today about the sex club is the most viewed feature on the Connections Web site in over three months. How can I go home when I'm finally turning the tide on this bad-luck wave that's been pulling me under for weeks?"

Damon fisted his hand around a bright blue sweater he'd tugged off a hanger. Clearly, he wasn't budging her without addressing her work issues first.

He lowered himself to the bed next to her feet.

"Why is this job so important to you?" He knew it went beyond a paycheck. "You carted that laptop on a blind date the first night we met, remember? Did you hope to sneak off to check your hit counter even then? Or write a blog about your date?"

"I wasn't working that night—"

"And what about the sex club? You visited that place even though you knew it could be dicey going in since a drug dealer recommended the spot. But you wouldn't back down because of your job. What gives?"

She pursed her lips in a thin, flat line. Thinking? Fuming? He didn't know. She was a tough woman to read.

"First of all, I believe my business is important. That may amuse you. But I've seen the results when people who felt totally 'undateable' in the mainstream bar scene come to Connections and find someone to love who loves them back."

Pulling off her glasses, she folded them and set them on the computer keyboard.

He was tempted to mention that while it was cool to help people fall in love, she could make the same contribution from anywhere. But she pinned him with her gaze and kept talking.

"That was me at one time. 'Undateable' according to the popular-culture standard. I was overweight and developed a speech impediment because my genius twin always did all the talking and I didn't have to. I was painfully shy because of both those things. I never learned how to flirt. Never even wanted to date since my mother married one man after another who turned out to be a loser."

Damon tried to see the woman she was describing and couldn't reconcile the image with what he saw now. He'd thought maybe she was uptight about her job, but perhaps that was just natural defensiveness from someone who'd obviously worked hard to create a healthy dating world through her career.

"What changed you?"

"Stepfather number three tried to molest me when I was seventeen. He saw the weight problem and the speech issues and pegged me for an easy mark."

Anger poured through him at the picture she painted. "He thought wrong."

"Not really." She shrugged, the old hurt rolling off her a hell of a lot easier than he could dismiss it. "I *was* insecure. My real father left when I was two, which I know now was a bruise on my heart throughout my whole childhood. But back then I hadn't figured it out yet. I just felt quietly unworthy."

He shook his head, refusing to accept her words. Hating that she was made to feel that way. "What happened to the stepfather?"

"Eventually he did a six-month jail term and paid off a massive civil suit from yours truly. But that was only after I fixed the speech problem, went to college and found myself under forty pounds of unhappiness."

He laid a hand on her ankle, needing to touch her. Connect with her.

"So you went into this business to create a more comfortable forum for people who might have a tough time meeting people otherwise." He could appreciate that better now. And for the first time, he saw something more vulnerable inside her that hadn't been apparent before.

Scratch that. He saw something vulnerable in her that she guarded with her smarts and determination. And yeah, that was something to admire.

"I liked thinking about what made couples a good fit. It was my way of rewriting my mother's past, since I wished she'd chosen a husband who cared about her and shared her values instead of a cute guy with enough cash to buy her a few baubles."

She eyed him across the bed, her gaze dark with emotions. "It's hard to see someone you love make one bad decision after another."

"I hear that." He said it adamantly enough that he realized he needed to follow up with some kind of an explanation. And damn, but he hadn't meant to go down that road anymore. Especially not with her.

A woman he'd already grown to care about too much.

She raised an eyebrow, her fingers slipping off the keyboard as she gave up any pretense of trying to work.

"I had a girlfriend—" As he started the story, it occurred to him he'd never told it before. Not to anyone in his stoic, quiet clan, and not even to Enrique, who knew a few details by default since he'd been stationed at Kodiak Air Station in Alaska when Kelly had left. "My live-in, actually. She walked out on me while I was stationed in Alaska, deciding out of the blue we were incompatible and that she needed someone more party oriented like her."

Lacey nodded, setting aside the laptop altogether. "She was doing her compatibility profiling a little late in the game, wasn't she?"

"I think the time alone in the middle of an Alaskan winter got to her. But yeah, she decided I was too much of a workaholic, and found somebody more fun. Or so she thought."

"She wasn't content with the next man, either?" Lacey frowned, and he could almost picture her inner matchmaker trying to compute why his relationship with Kelly didn't add up.

"I guess you could say that. After she called it quits

with me, Kelly moved south with some pond scum of a guy who'd gotten her hooked on drugs and then booted her out."

Lacey's eyes widened, clearly surprised at the turn the story had taken. Join the club. Maybe Damon should have been a little more careful about compatibility testing himself. And wasn't that a realization?

"Sometimes…" She cleared her throat and blinked. "Sometimes people have hurts that go far deeper than we can see on the surface." She brushed her fingers along the back of his hand.

Comforting. Wise.

He tried to steel himself against the warmth he felt inside, but it was too damn late. Her words soothed a raw place inside him.

"She had problems with her family—stuff I didn't really think about until after she left."

"I'm sorry she put you through that. Would you— Do you think you would have taken her back?" she asked softly, studying his face as if she might find answers to questions she hadn't asked yet.

"I honestly don't know." He'd thought about it more than once. "I know part of what drove her away was my job. Alaska alone could drive anyone off the deep end."

Lacey was quiet for a long moment. "You loved her."

The key word being *loved*. Past tense.

"Yeah, I did. But it's a damn rare relationship that can survive the Coast Guard, let alone thrive." He'd known that going in, but he'd taken a gamble with Kelly. A gamble that had hurt them both in the long run. "She's not the first person driven to desperate measures by Alaskan weather, eighteen hours of dark and a roommate whose job pulls him out of the sack at 3:00 a.m. to search for sinking boats."

He shook his head to clear it of old crap. He ought to be thinking about how to get Lacey out of town instead of the woman he'd already failed.

Still, Lacey didn't look ready to leave anytime soon. She'd kicked her shoes off, oblivious to the suitcase he'd put on the end of the bed or the laptop beside her. Instead she gazed at him with understanding in her eyes, not judging him for driving a woman into drug addiction.

How could he say goodbye to her right now when they were waist-deep in getting to know each other? The thought of losing his connection with her hurt more than he would have ever guessed.

"But that's ancient history." He didn't want to think about Kelly and all the ways he'd messed up in the past. "What about you? Anybody ever rip your heart out? Or have you managed to avoid that by only choosing guys you're compatible with?"

"Ha." She shook her head. "I'd be a whole lot richer if that were the case."

Tugging at the clasp of a rhinestone bracelet, she frowned at the catch that seemed to be stuck. He leaned closer, taking over the task until the purple stones slid free. Leaving them face-to-face on the bed. Close enough to kiss.

He dismissed the thought and straightened, unwilling to tangle his life with hers any more than necessary now that he knew she needed to leave. Soon. Memories of the briefing on Nick Castine left Damon with no doubt that the guy would come after Lacey again.

He would drug her like he'd drugged those other women unless Damon made sure she was safe. Protected.

"But I guess my heart has never really been all that broken," she admitted, long after he'd asked the question.

"Not really broken?" He had to laugh at that one. "It either is or it isn't, babe. There's no two ways about it."

She twined her fingers together and clenched her hands into a knot, a gesture that made him wonder if she wanted to touch him as badly as he wanted to touch her.

"There's a chance I might have held back a piece of myself to keep it safe," she said softly, her words falling into place with the rest of what he knew about her.

She wasn't uptight so much as protective. She'd kept him at arm's length all week except for when the chemistry had overpowered them both.

Reaching for her hands, he gently pried her fingers apart and laced his own through hers.

"I wish I was going to be there when you finally decide to let yourself go." He raised the back of her hand to his lips and kissed the soft skin, knowing his chances to touch her were dwindling, their time together almost over.

LACEY RECOGNIZED a goodbye when she heard one.

No matter that Damon said all the right things about wishing he could have a relationship, the bottom line was he wanted her out of Puerto Rico. Besides, he had to have some unresolved feelings for his former fiancée if she was still calling him.

That hurt. But maybe the pang she'd felt at discovering the identity of the woman who'd called Damon this morning was a clue that Lacey was in over her head. She should leave before things got any more serious with a man who wasn't ready for more. Plus, with all that she now knew about Nicholas Castine, she agreed she needed to be cautious.

Could she simply leave at a moment's notice the way he wanted her to? Put her work second for a change? Her sister kept telling her she couldn't allow her Web site to overshadow her whole life.

Of course, her work had saved her in so many ways after being abandoned by her father and overlooked by her mother in favor of one crappy stepfather after another. But maybe it had already provided all the personal growth it could. Perhaps it was time to heal the rest of her without that barrier getting in the way.

With the feel of Damon's kiss still tingling along the back of her hand, Lacey decided to put aside professional commitments and competitions and think about herself for a change.

She'd overcome a hell of a lot by testifying against the stepfather who'd touched her. No way would she put herself in a victim position again if she had anything to say about it.

"I'll leave tonight." She met his eyes, confident in the decision even though it meant walking away from Damon. "I've got a rental car to return and a few clothes to pack, but I could be on a flight by nine."

She had no idea how hard it would be to book something at the last minute, but flights to Miami were frequent out of San Juan.

"There's one at ten-fifteen. I checked on my way over here."

"Great. We've got one whole bonus hour to say goodbye." She hurt just thinking about it. After all the superficial relationships she'd maintained over long periods of time, the man who got around her barriers and under her skin turned out to be the man she'd known for the least amount of time.

She'd been toast from the very beginning.

"I know it's not ideal—"

"You're right. I'd rather not have any time to lie to each other and say we'll write when we both know this is the end." Standing, she unwound her fingers from his.

"I would never ask you to leave early if I didn't think you were at risk." He stood with her, blocking her path to the bathroom where her few travel supplies needed to be packed.

"I know."

"Do you?" He gripped her shoulders, his hands molding around bare skin and spaghetti straps.

The warmth she felt at his touch told her how much she'd come to care about him. She realized now, as she was faced with the prospect of saying goodbye, that Damon didn't need to fill out any stupid matchmaking profile for her to recognize how right they were together. Her subconscious had recognized a strong, honorable man long before the rest of her had figured it out. The kind of hot chemistry they shared wasn't some superficial by-product of overeager hormones. It was the intense side effect of her brain demanding she claim him before he slipped away.

"Yeah, I do." She knew without question that he would do whatever it took to protect her. And after being raised in such an unstable environment by a mother who didn't know how to safeguard her kids, there was something soul satisfying to realize the extent of Damon's commitment.

Even if he couldn't make a commitment to *her*.

"I don't want to say goodbye yet, either," he assured her, stroking his fingers down her shoulder blades and making her shiver with pleasure. "But we don't have a choice if we want to keep you safe."

"It would have been nice if we had more time." The wistful note in her voice gave her away, and she hoped he hadn't heard it.

His thumbs kept up their sensual assault on her back, and she realized—wise or unwise—she wanted this last hour with him. She needed one more time in his arms that wasn't tainted by drugs or fraught with worries that she was getting in too deep too fast.

She already knew she cared too much and there wasn't a damn thing she could do about it other than to enjoy these last stolen moments.

"I don't want to assume—" Damon slid one strap off her shoulder and leaned down to kiss the flesh he'd bared. "That is, if you have something else you need to do before you go—"

"There's nothing else I'd rather do." Not one damn thing. She'd rather be here—an active participant in breaking her own heart—than doing anything else right now. "Let's pretend we have all the time in the world."

Damon heard Lacey's request and vowed to make it his personal quest for the next sixty minutes. He'd insulted her job, booted her out of her first hotel and failed to protect her from the toxin in her drink. So being able to do this much for her would be a pleasure. One small way to make up for so many things that had gone wrong.

"If I had all the time in the world…" He unzipped

her dress, taking his time as the teeth unfastened, loosening the fabric around her curves. "I'd spend a hell of a lot of it just looking at you."

He sent the dress to the floor with a gentle nudge, soaking in the sight of her lavender silk bra and panties splashed with embroidered pink polka dots.

"Last night it was too dark to see anything." She tugged at the strap of the bra as if she wanted it off, but he wasn't done studying her.

Maybe if he watched her long enough he would figure out what it was that attracted him to her more than any other woman. If only he'd met her later—at the end of his commitment to the Coast Guard.

"If we had all the time in the world, I'd never make love to you in the dark again." His eyes roved over her, devouring her. She wasn't model thin. She was perfect. Curvy. Strong. Soft in all the best places.

His body strained with interest as she twitched restlessly, her fingers skimming the elastic of her underwear, following the waistline until she paused at her hip.

"That might be the nicest thing any man has ever said to me, Lieutenant." She slid her finger beneath the elastic, one shiny pink fingernail dipping into the silk until it emerged on the other end of the fabric.

Her eyes never left his face, but he couldn't hold her gaze. He watched her teasing seduction like a teen at his first strip club.

"I've got a lot more nice things to say," he assured her, his mouth going dry as she smoothed that seductive finger along her abdomen, the nail disappearing back into the triangle of fabric moving toward her mound. "What will a few more compliments buy me?"

She halted the tantalizing motion of her finger, never fully touching herself as her hand hovered just above her feminine center.

"I don't bargain away my favors," she chided, rolling her hips for his benefit. "I just like to feel inspired."

He didn't have a clue how to move her hand forward to where he wanted to see it, his creativity smoldering to ash as the temperature rose in the room.

"I'd sure like to know what it takes to inspire a hot blond bombshell in the midst of a striptease."

With her free hand, she reached out to stroke his chest. The front of his flight suit right down to his fly.

"I think a little visual stimulation is in order," she whispered, her voice a throaty purr that undid him as much as the words.

"Yes, ma'am," he agreed so fast his hands were on his zipper before she finished the request.

In the soft light of her hotel room, he observed her every movement, from the quick dip of her eyes to his lap to the rapid intake of breath that had her breasts testing the limits of her bra.

The woman was a walking, talking feast.

"That's better." She tucked her hand deeper into her panties, cupping her mound as her fingers cradled the flesh between her legs.

The knowledge that he did that to her—made her want to touch herself—finally healed that raw spot inside him that had festered since Kelly left. His ex might not have wanted to stick around for him, but Lacey didn't want to leave. She hungered for him so damn much she couldn't wait for his touch.

He shucked off his flight suit and ditched his T-shirt.

Pulling her to him, he relished the feel of her against his skin. Her eyes opened wide, their gazes connecting for one sizzling second before he tugged her hand free of its place between her legs. Then, his eyes never leaving hers, he tasted each of her fingers with thorough sweeps of his tongue.

Her knees went out from under her as she fell into him, her breasts spilling over the top of her bra to tease along his chest. The sensory input was enough to make him explode. The sweet scent of her drove him crazy, demanding he find the source of that taste.

Backing her up to the bed, he pulled her legs out from under her until she fell into the mattress. He cushioned her fall with his arms, settling her onto the spread so her legs dangled off the edge. With impatient hands, he peeled away her panties then, positioning himself between her thighs, he kissed her intimately. Slowly. Thoroughly.

Her hands traveled over his shoulders at first, but as he deepened the kiss and quickened his pace, they fell away. She sighed and twisted beneath him, her breathy sounds making him want her more. He pressed harder, gripping her thighs to steady her right where he needed her.

She bucked underneath him, her hips rolling and thrashing as her legs trembled. He slowed down enough to slide one finger deep inside her. And then a second. She was drenched and shaking when he flicked his tongue against the tight center of her. Her gasp warned him he'd hit the right note in the moment before she tensed. Cried out.

Her whole body shuddered with the force of her release and he savored every sensual spasm. The tremors went on and on, her nails raking over his shoulders as her heels pressed into his back. Not until she stilled again did he release her, his body on fire and rock solid, ready for hers.

"Come here," he guided her, sitting down on the bed before he helped her to sit on his lap, facing him.

"I don't know where I put the condoms," she fretted, her eyes unfocused as she peered around the hotel room.

"I've got them." He'd been the last one to use them, after all. "They're right here."

He'd stashed the box next to the bed, and, reaching down, he removed one from the packaging. His boxers were only half-off, landing somewhere around his knees as they'd shuffled down onto the bed. But he didn't care. Nothing mattered except for being with Lacey right now.

Apparently she thought the same thing. She pulled the condom from his hand and rolled it on, freeing him to cup her breasts and mold them to his hands. He raked her hips closer to his, pulling her up his thighs until the wet heat of her cradled his cock, setting his blood on fire. He lifted her up, positioning her at the tip of his shaft and then easing her down in slow, amazing degrees.

The feel of her around him drove him insane. And having her there, nose to nose, mouth to mouth with him made him keenly aware of her as a woman and not just a hot sex partner. Lacey was spending her last hour in tropical paradise here. With him. Taking him deep inside her and giving him more pleasure than he'd ever imagined.

Giving himself over to sensation, he shut down everything else to focus on the moment. Her. He wrapped her up in his arms and pressed his lips to hers, taking everything she had. She locked her ankles around his waist and held on, the tone of her urgent little sighs telling him she was close to finding release all over again. Heat slicked his back with sweat, the ocean air blowing in off the water keeping the room sultry. Lacey's fingers dug into his shoulders, holding him tight as her back arched and her hips ground into his.

Then his release hit him like a killer wave, pulling him under and down as sensation swamped him. He hadn't expected it to hit so fast, but he couldn't hold back, not even when he felt Lacey's fingernails dig deep into his arms and her sex tighten around him in the moments before orgasm. He just had to hope he didn't break her rhythm...

And then she shuddered once, twice, three times. Her body trembled with lush spasms as she found her peak and rode it out right alongside him.

The scent of her filled his nostrils and he buried his head in her hair. His heart beat erratically, filling his ears with the sound of how off-kilter she made him.

Logically he knew he ought to release her and help her get to the airport. The sooner she was out of Puerto Rico, the faster he'd be able to make his bust and ensure Castine never drugged anyone else. But with the alarm clock beside the bed illuminating the small window of time before they had to leave, Damon couldn't stand to relinquish his hold on her just yet.

"Lacey?" His voice rasped as if he hadn't used it. Or as if he'd just shouted himself hoarse, a more likely scenario.

"Mmm?" She flexed her toes behind his back, her muscles stretching against his sides. Still, she didn't pick her head up from where it rested on his shoulder.

"Lie here with me." He leaned back, bringing her down to the mattress with him. "Just for a minute."

Or two. Or a lifetime.

He didn't know where the idea had come from, but he shut it down. He wouldn't let regrets about what might have been ruin the here and now.

"That was amazing," she whispered in his ear, their bodies still joined. "I wish I didn't have to leave."

He couldn't speak, didn't know how to express the firestorm she'd unleashed in him. All he knew was that the clock was ticking on their time together and once Lacey left, his world wouldn't go back to being as dull and gray as it had been before she'd arrived.

No. It would be worse, since now he would know exactly what he was missing.

12

LIKE ANY MATURE ADULT LACEY held back the tears until she got home.

She'd planned for the emotional breakdown from the moment she'd blundered through a hasty airport goodbye to Damon before stepping on the direct flight from San Juan to Miami. She hadn't even let the tears fall in the privacy of her earth-friendly hybrid vehicle that Laura had talked her into last year. If she'd let the emotions flow in the car, she might have compromised her driving ability on the dark roads that led to a narrow causeway joining the mainland and one of the bigger islands. And she'd needed her wits about her to make the ferry that crossed to the more remote islands. As it was, she'd had to bribe the ferry operator a hefty sum to take her back home at the unusual hour.

Now, walking into the quiet house that was her escape from the world, Lacey unlocked the barrier on her emotions. She dropped onto a stool at the kitchen island, not bothering to take her shoes off, and cried out her frustration.

She cried over her business because she had struggled so hard and still met with meager success, and because she'd finally found some success and then had to walk away from the source of material for her newly popular blog.

Mostly she cried over leaving Damon Craig.

Walking away from him had hurt. The pain in her chest radiated through her whole body as she collapsed onto the granite countertop. Tears fell unchecked onto the smooth surface. She would have never guessed she would grow to care about anyone so quickly. So deeply.

But that's what had happened with Damon. It didn't matter that she wanted to fall for someone *after* she'd secured professional success. Or that she planned to find happiness with someone whose characteristics helped her see in black-and-white print that they were meant to be together. She'd fallen for a stranger in a bar and made out with him on the beach before she knew jack squat about him.

And things had only gotten better from there. She'd somehow forged the most compelling relationship of her life while ignoring everything she'd thought she understood about dating. She felt like a professional fraud.

Yanking a clean dish towel off a shelf beneath the island countertop, Lacey swiped the cotton over her face to dry her tears and get a grip. She had no idea how she was going to recover from the heartache she'd been putting off her whole adult life, but now that she was in the thick of it, she realized she was glad she hadn't avoided it this time. Life without feeling deeply was an existence only half-lived. And she wouldn't trade her days with Damon for anything—not even the opportunity to erase the hurt inside her right now.

Lifting her head from the granite, Lacey saw the world around her with new eyes. Her isolation. Her remote home that had felt like a retreat just last week suddenly seemed confining. Restricting her from finding happiness by wrapping her in total privacy.

The surroundings appeared the same but different. Take for example the glass of water in the middle of the counter. She sure didn't remember setting it there before she left. But now it sat there, reflecting the moonlight coming in off the water just outside the French doors.

Why would she have poured a full glass and left it there?

She set down the dish towel, a hairy sensation crawling down her neck. Turning to take stock of the rest of the house, she searched for things amiss, like the man stepping from the shadows.

"Why so sad, Lacey?"

Nicholas Castine stood in her living room, fifteen feet away. He held a gun in his right hand, the barrel pointed at her. Rumpled and unshaven, he bore little resemblance to the slick, smooth-talking businessman she'd met at Rosita's Café last Friday night. Or maybe it was just that she now knew he was a drug dealer. Potentially violent. A sex addict who had followed her a thousand miles to her home.

She tried to speak, but her voice didn't come. Fear quivered through her and froze her in place.

"I see I've startled you." He smiled like a man genuinely enjoying himself. "It would have been so much easier if we could have coordinated schedules while you were in San Juan."

Lacey struggled to lock down her fear and remember some basic rules of human nature. She didn't want to alienate him or make him mad. If he wanted to pretend they were friends who couldn't "coordinate schedules," that was fine by her. With a supreme effort she found her voice.

"I had a work emergency," she lied, hoping to draw the conversation away from their date. "Computer problems."

Her voice sounded thin. Terrified. But for the life of her, she couldn't turn up the volume. Her heart beat fast and erratically, shaking her from the inside out.

How had he gotten here? Did Damon know?

Her chest ached with the sudden realization that she'd never told Damon how she felt about him.

"Lucky for me, the El San Juan Hotel had this address on file for you." He gestured to her home as he took two steps closer. "Nice place you have here."

She backed up to the island, wishing the knife drawer was a whole lot closer. She couldn't think of anything to fight him with. For that matter, even if she got away from him, where would she go? Her home was the only residence on the tiny island well off the mainland.

"It's not quite as private as I would like between the boat patrols and the developers creating their own little islands all around me to accommodate buyers." She sidestepped along the counter, feeling around behind her for anything in the recessed shelves that she could use as a weapon.

"It seems private enough for my needs, but then, we won't be here very long." He closed the distance between them to stand face-to-face with her, the gun between them.

He smelled like sweat and expensive cologne, a combination that made her want to throw up.

"We?" She couldn't help but wonder what plans he

had for her. Hadn't she read somewhere that being moved from the scene of a crime increased your chances of dying astronomically? If he moved her, she was as good as dead.

"My associates and I." He leaned close to her and she sucked in a breath to avoid contact.

But at the last minute, he merely reached past her and picked up the glass of water that she'd noticed on the counter earlier.

"Can I get you a drink?" He waved the glass under her nose like a tempting treat.

And still, the bastard smiled.

"Drugs don't agree with my system." She clutched her stomach meaningfully. "I'd better not or I'll be retching up my guts all night."

An old memory returned to her as she recalled telling her third stepfather the same thing when he'd tried to get her drunk on her seventeenth birthday. Oddly, she felt more in control now—even with a gun pointed at her navel—than she had back then when she'd had no faith in herself. She was smarter now. Stronger.

"But maybe one of your associates would like it?" she offered, wondering how many other people could possibly be in the house or on the island. "I could make some sandwiches. You must be starving after your long flight."

She stepped toward the refrigerator, but he set down the water and gripped her arm with a steely strength she hadn't expected in a man so lean.

"I don't think so, Lacey." Yanking her closer, he set down the gun on the island to restrain her with both hands. "You and I have unfinished business."

He held her tight against him, the scent of his sweat

and his man-whore perfume turning her stomach. "We're going to address that before I put this property to work for me as a drop-off point. Have I told you that you have excellent taste in drug-lord hideouts?"

He reached for her blouse with no warning and, gripping the collar, shredded it with one violent tear. Lacey screamed in surprise, seeing his mood swing from congenial to lethal in an instant.

Cool air filtering in through the French doors hit her bared skin like a splash of icy reality. This man would hurt her, body and soul. And then he'd kill her. ·

She saw it in his eyes.

Seizing her chance while the gun lay idle, Lacey kneed him in the balls. Jammed her fingers into his eye socket.

Then she ran like hell.

Castine's screams echoed in her ears—almost as loud as her own shrieks for help—as she hit the deck outside the French doors. Already she heard other men's voices nearby. The associates.

Help me, God.

She ran across the grass toward the water, away from the dock slip where she saw the shape of a foreign water craft. She had almost hit the surf when a gunshot rang out in the night.

DAMON HATED riding shotgun even under the best circumstances. Tonight ranked as the twelfth circle of hell.

"Where the fuck is her house?" He pored over the navigational maps in the back of an H65-A Dolphin helicopter out of Miami.

While he'd been with Lacey, one of Castine's aliases had popped up on a commercial flight to Miami. The

9:00 p.m. out of San Juan that Lacey had skipped in favor of the 10:15.

The lead had raised red flags about the intelligence they'd received about the region around Rincon, alerting the Coast Guard's Deployable Operations Group that the barge off the northwest tip of Puerto Rico was most likely a decoy. Damon hadn't waited for permission to launch an op, knowing Stafford would have shot down the timetable. Instead, he'd tapped a friend with a private airstrip and flown to Miami himself.

But U.S. Coast Guard resources at the air station in Miami had required he take a back seat. Having command of the op didn't mean he could fly it.

Still, the hotshot new guy at the controls of the chopper—the same aircraft Damon had flown every day of his career for the past three years—seemed to know what he was doing. If only the damned navigational maps showed the island that Lacey called home.

"I know this place," the pilot yelled back through the headset to where Damon was forced to cool his heels in the cargo bay. "Every high-end developer in the world wants to sell private islands. Now that they've got the technology, these suckers are popping up faster than the maps can keep up with."

Damon strapped on diving gear, as did a search-and-rescue seaman who would back him up. He didn't know what they'd find at Lacey's place, but he would be prepared either way. Two of the Miami fleet's fastest cutters were on their way out to the island, while another short-range-recovery helicopter waited on standby if they needed help. Damon's gut told him that Castine had planned on shipping his drugs out using Lacey's house as a checkpoint to break up the larger payload into smaller parcels. Targeting Lacey's matchmaking system had only been a sideline bonus to a bigger plan all along.

He kept the headset on while the pilot on the Miami-based helicopter slowed the engines, needing to hear any last communications before he strapped on the dive mask.

He hadn't been in the water for a while, since he was usually the one at the controls. But for Lacey he'd take the plunge into the Atlantic himself.

"Your friend has company, Lieutenant." The copilot's voice came through the headset, his Southern accent as thick as Enrique's. "I see two unidentified vessels in the slip and a cigarette boat—about a forty-footer—anchored about a hundred yards off to the east."

The seaman in the dive gear pulled open the door as the aircraft slowed, allowing Damon's eyes to roam over the inky water below. The winds were calm tonight, the chopper blades kicking up the majority of the air whipping around the cargo area.

"Good. That means she's still there." Damon didn't need to explain who "she" was. Every man on board knew he wasn't flying like a bat out of hell up the east coast just to stop a drug shipment.

The drugs allowed him to tap the Coast Guard. The woman fueled his every step. All these years when he'd put his job first were going to be paid back right now, when he needed to put Lacey before everything else. He wouldn't let Castine touch her, and if that meant the drug runner ate a bullet tonight instead of standing trial in federal court, that was exactly what was going down.

Lacey had shown Damon a level of trust no woman had ever given him before, an honest piece of herself despite her own tendency to guard her heart. And she hadn't shown her caring by giving up her career to follow him around the country for his job. Instead she'd held on to her work and the things that made her unique, the same way he always had. If one of them didn't bend, they'd never be together. He didn't know how to reconcile that, but he damn well had discovered in the past twenty-four hours that he would like to try. Women with Lacey's strength and independence—whether she recognized it in herself or not—didn't come along every day.

"Sir, I suggest we wait for the cutters to provide backup if this thing goes bad." The hotshot set the aircraft to automatic flight control before he wrenched around in his seat to see Damon. "I can hover at fifty feet and wait for you, but you know I've got to get my ass back in the sky if those boats start shooting."

"Affirmative." Damon ripped off the headset and tugged on the mask, refusing to think he might be too late. "Half your fleet's going to be in the water out here before dawn. I'll get a ride home somehow."

Flashing the thumb's-up signal, Damon jumped out the side into the blackness below to find the woman he'd already fallen for.

BLOOD LOSS SLOWED her steps.

Lacey could hear Nicholas gaining on her, his footsteps pounding on the damp ground behind her. His footfalls echoed faster than hers.

The bullet had only grazed her, but the red-hot sting across her flesh had brought her to her knees. Not bothering to check it, she had scrambled to her feet and run toward the old boathouse, knowing she couldn't swim with this wound or she'd lose too much blood too fast. The minor injury could turn deadly too easily.

"You really should just take the drug, Lacey." Castine's voice was suddenly in her ear, his sweaty stink filling her nostrils while her head swam. "You'll feel better. Remember how good you felt at In the Flesh while you were on the dance floor?"

She felt his arms around her, lowering her to the ground. Wet grass clung to her back while her vision narrowed to Castine's thin, haggard face above her. Still smiling, the ugly bastard.

"Get off me," she snarled, furious to think he would touch her while she bled like a stuck pig, unable to defend herself.

"So fiery." He rested more of his weight on her, a nauseating erection jabbing her leg. "You just need to take the medicine and feel better."

He jabbed a pill between her lips, rousing another bout of fury. She couldn't win this battle; she knew it deep inside. But she would fight until she was unconscious or dead, because she wouldn't be able to deal with the aftermath otherwise. She understood that about herself now.

She was no man's victim.

Spitting the pill as far as it would go, it was her turn to smile as Castine cursed like a lunatic. She wanted to piss him off to the very last second, to make sure he knew he'd picked the wrong woman to mess with.

In slow motion she watched him raise his hand to her. The lack of blood flow made the moment feel surreal and she wondered if she was dying. Her head throbbed. Her heartbeat was slow, but each pulse ached more than the last.

Maybe she'd taken some of the drug after all. She closed her eyes and waited for the blow, too tired to fight anymore.

A harsh gurgling noise came instead.

Pulling her eyes open, she saw Nicholas Castine with a knife in his chest. Above him, Damon stood dark and dripping like Poseidon come to land for a reckoning.

He hauled Castine away from her like so much refuse, the man who'd shot her a threat no more. Gratitude exploded in her chest, filling her insides with hope and joy despite the blood leeching thought and life from her body.

"I want you to know I love you." Lacey was so happy he was there to hear it. If she died tonight—and she prayed that wasn't even a remote possibility—she would rest a little easier knowing something very important had been said.

She wasn't holding back on life, or love, ever again.

13

ACCORDING TO the Coast Guard press release the next morning, the news was all about the pounds of drugs seized, the street value of the goods and the number of arrests made.

But as Damon waited for the E.R. docs to release Lacey, he had another take on the successes of the night. Lacey was going to be okay.

And really, that was all that mattered.

He braced his head on his hands, his elbows on his knees as he tried to squeeze the image from his mind of her turning white from blood loss on the beach. Her breath had hitched oddly. Her words had slowed.

But the ones she chose to say before she slipped into unconsciousness…that part he didn't want to forget. She'd entrusted him with something more precious than he deserved. She loved him even though he'd sent her away without any plans to ever see her again.

The confession awed him. Humbled him. Made him realize he'd made Lacey pay for the trust issues someone else had foisted on him.

"You must be the boyfriend from Puerto Rico." A

woman's voice barked down at him from above, drawing Damon out of his thoughts. He looked up to see an endlessly tall blonde in Birkenstocks and a pink tie-dyed skirt, carrying a poodle. "The one who bolted the last time my twin was under a doctor's care. You can feel free to dash, now that I'm here."

Damon wanted to set her straight, but she pivoted on her heel and took off for the nurses' station, already calling to one of the people in scrubs around the desk.

"I'm next of kin for Lacey Sutherland. Could I speak to someone about her condition?" She tucked her little dog into a carrier that looked like a handbag, effectively smuggling the furry mutt past the No Pets sign.

"Hold up." Damon found his voice and shot to his feet, but not before a nurse had reeled off Lacey's condition and assured the other woman that her sister would be released shortly.

The woman turned back to him. Her blue eyes were similar to Lacey's, but the resemblance ended there. Where Lacey was curvy, this woman looked more like an American Gladiator. Her long hair was darker than Lacey's, each strand arrow straight, her bangs cut straight across her head.

"Still here?" She smirked at him with the smart-ass attitude of a woman who wanted to fight. But then, her sister had been shot and she probably thought he was to blame.

Perhaps not without reason.

"I'm not going anywhere." He extended his hand, hoping to get off on a better foot. "Damon Craig."

"Laura Sutherland." She ignored his hand. "And why should I trust a man who left my sister in an E.R.

once before after a drug trip? Her first and only, I might add?"

"I left during a follow-up visit the next day because I thought I had the chance to nail the bastard who gave her the drugs in the first place." Had he made a bad call? "I was worried he would come after her again if I didn't track him down."

Laura looked thoughtful. Her little dog barked inside its denim carrier. Heads turned in the waiting room, looking for the source of the sound while Laura appeared oblivious.

"But you failed to stop him." Laura's expression lost some of its haughty coolness as a hint of fear showed through. "He shot her. She could have *died*."

The thought chilled him all over again. He'd spent hours in a wet flight suit after he'd brought her here, but even now that he was dry, the memory of what could have happened—of how close she'd come to death—froze him inside.

"I did everything in my power to make sure that didn't happen." And still it almost hadn't been enough. If the Dolphin helicopter pilot had been even a fraction of a second slower…

"Is it true the man is dead?" Laura lowered her voice and pulled a dog bone out of her purse before passing it into the carrier.

"Yes." His eyes went to a nurse in purple scrubs pushing through a set of double doors at the end of the hall. Lacey's nurse. "He won't bother her again."

"Lieutenant Craig?" The silver-haired nurse waved him toward the doors. "The doctor is finished with her. You can take her home now."

"Thank you." He crossed the waiting room with Laura at his side, then held the door for her.

Would Lacey remember what she'd said to him the night before? He'd seen her briefly after the docs stitched her up, but then he'd had to meet with members of his team who'd finished out the op without him. He'd taken an unconscious Lacey to the boathouse until it was safe for the helicopter to pick them up, unwilling to expose her to any of Castine's crew until the cutters were in position to board the boats. Damon had stanched the bleeding and kept her warm for the next ten minutes that felt like hours. He hadn't reported for an official debrief, but his connection with Lacey had bought him some time. He'd filed basic paperwork on a laptop Enrique had brought to the hospital for him while she'd slept.

Damon followed the nurse to Lacey's room, turning down a maze of hallways threading throughout multiple wings. She sat up in bed, the color returned to her cheeks. The blue hospital gown gaped around her shoulders, the material slipping down one arm while she edged closer to the side of the bed.

"Thank God you're here."

For a moment, he thought the greeting was for him, but Lacey pointed a finger at her sister. "Please say you brought clothes."

Damon regretted not thinking of it himself. Her shirt had been torn off her by the son of a bitch who'd wanted to hurt her. Damon had nearly lost his mind thinking about what a nightmare she'd been through.

Was still going through. No doubt the memories of what had happened would haunt her for a while.

"Of course." Laura hurried over to the bed and

dropped her purse, the dog carrier and a backpack on the mattress. "To show my love, I didn't even torment you with a Grateful Dead T-shirt. See?"

Lacey snapped up the white tank top and a pair of blue shorts.

"Endlessly thoughtful of you. Will you help me change?" She directed that request to Laura, as well, making him feel like an intruder when he just wanted to scoop her up and steal her away from everyone.

But if he was going to make a case that they should try being together, he didn't want her to think he would take her away from her family and her friends. His job had a way of doing that with no help from him.

He stepped out of the room and shut the door behind him to give Lacey privacy. What would it be like to spend time with her that wasn't for the sake of protecting her? Would she welcome his presence in her life, or had her half-conscious confession been a fanciful rambling in her gratitude for being saved?

"Come on in, big guy." Laura hauled open the door and waved to him, her poodle in her arms. "She wants to see you."

Damon turned to see her, knowing this might be his only chance to say the right things and prove to Lacey he was a good match for her after all.

LACEY HAD NEVER BEEN SO nervous.

How did a woman thank the man who saved her life? A man she now knew she loved, even though he didn't seem to want any part of a deeper relationship?

"Look, kiddies." Laura packed up Lacey's torn clothes and personal belongings in one of the hospital bags. "How about I head out to the island to see what I can clean up before you come home? Maybe Captain America can get you settled into a hotel nearby until the house is ready."

Lacey stifled a grin, wondering how Damon would deal with her bossy twin.

"She'll be in good hands," he assured Laura, not appearing fazed in the least to take orders from a six-foot girl bully.

In fact, Damon eyed Lacey with the intent stare of a man who wanted to be alone with her. Soon.

Her heart picked up speed in spite of everything she'd been through.

"Yes, well, just bear in mind she needs *rest* and recovery." Laura held Brillo out to Lacey for her to pet before she stashed him in his carrier. "I've got my eye on you, Lieutenant Craig."

Damon nodded.

When he didn't speak, Laura arched up on her toes the extra inch or two needed to reach Damon's cheek. She planted a kiss on his jaw.

"Thank you for protecting my baby sister." And with that, she plowed out the door, shoving it wide to make way for her and all her bags, a tornado of determination.

Leaving the room suddenly very, very quiet.

"You saved me," Lacey remarked, needing to fill the silence and address the huge thing that he'd done for her. "I've never been so scared in all my life."

He moved closer to her, his flight suit wrinkled and stiff from his time in the water the night before. It all seemed surreal today. God, he'd been a sight to behold when he'd appeared out of nowhere, dripping with anger and the sea.

"But you didn't let that stop you from fighting." He sat down on the bed beside her, his presence enough to make something glow inside her. "I saw you jabbed him in the eyes."

"I wasn't going to let him hurt me without a battle." Her old insecurities were part of her past—ghosts she didn't have to worry about anymore. "But he would have won if you hadn't arrived. How did you know he was here?"

"My team got word that one of Castine's aliases was used on the flight to Miami that left before yours last night. I heard about it a few minutes after your plane was in the air so I borrowed a friend's plane to get to the mainland while I waited for approval to coordinate an interdiction flight out of the Miami base." He picked up her hand and carefully lined up their palms. Turning his hand two degrees clockwise, he threaded their fingers together, filling all the valleys with his strength.

"He brought his drugs and his boats with him." She hadn't been able to process it all last night, but this morning she'd woken up with the need to fill in the blanks. "Do you think he planned to use my house as a drop-off point all along?"

She studied his face in the afternoon sun slanting through the white hospital blinds. His jaw dark with stubble. The slash of a depression perfectly centered in his chin. Dressed in his flight suit with the Coast Guard's *Semper Paratus* Always Ready patch stitched on his chest, he could have been the poster face for the armed forces. There was something fearless and noble etched in the lines around his eyes, but maybe she only saw that because she'd been a witness to what this man could do.

"I think that was dumb luck on his part, but maybe

I'm underestimating the guy. My guess is that he was only interested in using the matchmaking site to meet women, and discovered the convenience of your place as a distribution point later. The police will be in touch with you to gather evidence from your company's computer records."

"I don't have a company anymore." She wanted him to be the first to know, the first to see the changes she planned for her life, since knowing him had been the impetus for her new perspectives on so many things.

"You're abandoning Connections?" He turned to face her, and she could tell she'd surprised him.

"I typed a farewell letter to my members on the plane ride to Miami last night and I'll post it when I get home." Sliding her fingers free of his, she rose up off the bed, afraid if she sat by him too long she'd never be able to pry herself away. Leaving him once had been tough enough. She didn't trust herself to have the strength to do it a second time, especially when her emotions were still so raw after the roller coaster of the past twenty-four hours. But she didn't deceive herself that he'd be leaving the Coast Guard to hang out with her in Florida anytime soon.

He stood beside her, his eyebrows drawn in concern. For her? Or would he have this same protective urge toward any woman whose life he'd saved?

"Why?" He pulled a crumpled piece of paper from his pocket, the weathered sheet stained with ink smudges as if it had gone into the water along with the rest of him the night before. "I finished the rest of that dating profile you gave me. I thought it was insightful."

He smoothed his hand over the crinkles, as if he

could will away the damage done. She smiled, touched that he had tried to fit himself into her world. Outside her hospital room, an emergency team wheeled a gurney past, their feet pounding down the ceramic tile as nurses and doctors shouted orders.

The quiet in the aftermath seemed all the more silent.

"I've learned that sometimes we don't know what we are looking for until we find it." Her heart ached with the truth of that knowledge since she was looking at the kind of man she wanted. The kind of man she loved no matter how they matched up on paper. "If the profiles are helpful at all, I think their best use is to know ourselves before we can really be ready to seek someone else."

She swept her discharge papers off the side table near the hospital bed and folded them under her arm. Damon stared at her like he didn't know her.

And maybe he didn't.

She didn't feel like the same woman she'd been a week ago.

"I'm ready to leave if you are," she prompted, unsure what he would do with her after they left the hospital. "I can get a room at the Fontainebleau until my sister has the house cleaned up. I've always wanted to stay there, but never had a reason until now."

She tucked her finger in her pocket where she'd transferred the little piece of quartz crystal Tatiana had given her for good luck. No matter that the jewelry maker had been a small-time dealer on the side. She'd known a few things about life that Lacey hadn't, and one of them was about taking time to experience beauty. Joy.

Or maybe Tatiana had seen the similarity between Lacey and that rough piece of crystal? They might have started off hidden from the world, but with a polishing, they'd sparkle just fine.

She'd told Damon that she loved him, and she refused to regret taking that risk even if he didn't appear to return the sentiment. The only thing for her to do now was to pursue her own happiness and try not to let this first failed attempt dissuade her from a new path in life. A fresh start.

She might be stronger and wiser, but she had her first broken heart to tend and she suspected the healing of that wound would be far slower than the gash on her leg.

A COUNTEROFFENSIVE was needed and he was the man for the job.

Tension tightened Damon's shoulders as he drove down Ocean Drive toward South Beach's art deco district. The pilot who'd flown him out to Lacey's place had proven a stand-up guy and had dropped off an old truck at the hospital the night before for Damon to use while he was in town. The hours in the E.R. waiting room had been a blur, but the guy had left the keys at the nurses' station while Lacey was getting stitched up. He'd left a note telling Damon to enjoy being behind the controls.

The gesture reminded him that although military life sucked for couples, people in uniform recognized the high toll it took and they tried to support whatever relationships managed to take root. Tejal had come running when Damon needed a doctor for Lacey in Puerto

Rico, and the hotshot pilot based in Miami didn't know Damon from Adam, but he'd ponied up a personal vehicle to help out another flyer.

All of which gave him the confidence to take another shot at the impossible. This time he'd take the chance with a woman as tough and stubborn as he was.

"I think the Fontainebleau's in the other direction." Lacey swiveled in her seat to peer out the rear window of the beat-up old truck. "Yes. I see it back there."

Damon geared up for his next campaign. Deep breath.

"Actually, there was no room at the VOQ on base here, so I have a suite at the Roxy just down the road." He pointed up the street to one of the funky art deco buildings. "It's no Fontainebleau, but it's got all the amenities. Plus I'd be around if you need anything."

"You don't need to feel obligated to me forever." Her voice was distant. Cool. "You already saved me."

He'd forgotten how prickly she could be. Independent. Even her matchmaking profile about her said as much, and yeah, he'd finally gotten around to reading it. When launching a counteroffensive, a warrior needed to leverage all possible weapons.

And, damn it, he was fighting for both of them.

"What if what I feel goes beyond obligation?" He steered the truck into the Roxy's parking lot since she hadn't told him to turn around. He would honor her wishes—and take his own room next to hers at the Fountainebleau, if necessary. But she'd have to voice them first.

"Look." She didn't move when he put the truck in Park. Instead, she remained in her seat, her arms folded over the white T-shirt her sister had given her. "I understand that you've been burned before and that you're not ready for a major commitment at this point in your life. But I've realized that I am. And I've passed the point of no return with you, so I can't afford to lose any more of my heart to a man who is unprepared to give me any of his."

He switched off the ignition, measuring words that might be the most important ones he ever spoke. God, he hoped he got it right.

"But I am prepared." Unbuckling his seat belt, he slid closer to her on the bench seat. "I wanted to wait to speak to you alone. Hell, I've been waiting all night for the right time, but there've been docs stitching you up and nurses doling out medicines and an overbearing twin sister telling me to take a hike."

Lacey didn't soften her stance in the corner of the truck, but one side of her mouth kicked up at the mention of Laura.

"She was my watchdog long before you."

"No doubt she's twice as vigilant since your stepfather, so I'll cut her some slack." He leaned closer and unfastened Lacey's seat belt, too, careful to be gentle around a body that had to be bruised and sore. "But I'm not trying to be a watchdog anymore. I'm trying to tell you I can't ignore what I feel for you just because I'm not sure how to make it work."

Her lips pursed in thought, the plump curve of her mouth making him want to kiss her. To communicate with her in the most elemental of ways.

"What do you mean?"

"I mean I love you." He dusted off the words he'd thought he wouldn't say again for a long time. "I didn't spout all that stuff about attraction just for the hell of it that night we met. I believe that. And I didn't date a soul for a whole year, because I didn't feel that with anyone else. But whether it was convenient or not, I felt it with you in about two seconds after I saw you."

Her arms unfolded and she straightened against the seat. Was that progress? Hope kicked to life.

"But what about your ex-girlfriend?" Her blue eyes remained guarded. Wary. "I couldn't help but overhear that she called you recently. And I know you weren't sure if you'd take her back…"

"Whoa." Had he said that? "I might not have been sure at the time—like in those first few weeks after she left. But that was a long time ago. The only reason she called me this week was to mislead me about the whereabouts of Castine's drug shipment. He must have paid her to give me the runaround once he knew I was getting close. There's a good chance she'll be going to prison for tampering with a federal investigation."

All of this seemed to surprise Lacey, reminding him all over again how hard his job would be on them.

"I thought you still spoke to her. That you might still care for her." The anguish showed in her eyes and, as much as he hated putting it there, he saw the truth of how she felt about him, too. And that meant as much to him as any words ever could.

"I'm so sorry, Lacey." He reached for her, carefully, and wrapped his arms around her. "You see why my job is hell on relationships? I wasn't at liberty to say much about what I was doing."

She nodded against his shoulder, her cheek warm and sweet along his chest.

"Yes, but how often will an ex-girlfriend be involved

in your work?" She leaned back to peer up at him. "I think I could handle anything else as long as I knew that you and I were solid."

Relief blew through him like the warm breeze wafting through the truck windows.

"I could transfer to the Miami station if it would help." He couldn't give up the job that was so much a part of him, but he could adjust it. Mold it to fit into their lives so they could be together. "I'd still have to be on alert most nights. And I might disappear at three in the morning to go pull people out of the water."

"I think what you do is amazing." She smiled, and he felt like a freaking superhero.

"I think what you do is pretty damn cool, too. I hate to see you walk away from something you're so good at. I can save lives while you save relationships."

"I'm still going to do that." She lifted her hands to his shoulders, her touch so sweet he closed his eyes for a moment to soak in the pleasure it brought. "I've been talking to my sister a little more and I think we're going to team up to develop a joint matchmaking site, perhaps with a self-awareness component to help members understand themselves better before they start searching for true love."

"The old enemies turned joint forces?" He could easily see the two of them taking on the world. "Even with such different points of view?"

"Not so different, maybe." Her fingers trailed up his collar to skim along his neck. "I think I've seen some of the wisdom in how she tries to help people. And I think I can do more with all the data her mathematical brain has to offer. I'm the organized one, you know."

She grinned and he joined her, liking the idea of her finding peace with at least one member of her family.

"Sounds like you'll be busy for a while."

"As if you won't be? Who knows where you'll be jetting off to next. We can't pretend our jobs aren't a big part of who we are, but we could try to tame them into more manageable pieces of ourselves so they don't rob us of downtime. Leisure time."

She stroked the underside of his jaw with the smooth caress of one fingernail. The touch resonated clear down to his toes, reminding him how much he wanted to get her upstairs where they could be alone.

"Pleasure time," he clarified, seeing a whole lot of that in his future.

"Exactly."

He caught her roaming finger in his hand and kissed it, his whole body humming with the promise of good things to come.

"So as a professional matchmaker, what do you think the odds are for us, knowing that military life is hell on couples?"

"Do you remember how hard I fought last night to get free of Castine?" Her voice turned serious, her blue eyes shifting a shade darker.

The memory twisted his gut.

"I'm so sorry you had to go through that." He would have traded anything to be there faster. To have prevented her from that fear and pain.

"Don't be." Her voice was strong and unrepentant. "I'm not. Because I learned that I can take whatever life dishes out. I can fight for my happy endings and win."

Damon heard the confidence in her voice and grinned.

"I believe you can."

"And while we're on the subject of our future, I hope you'll consider staying put in Puerto Rico for a little longer." She tipped her forehead to his, her body brushing tantalizingly close.

"Really?" He'd already been thinking about what he needed to do to relocate.

"I hardly got to see it on my vacation. And a friend told me I should take my time to enjoy paradise." She kissed his cheek and nipped his ear, revving his pulse and prompting him to pry open the truck door.

Time to claim that happy ending in the privacy of his suite.

"Can do." He practically sprinted around to the passenger's door to retrieve her, unwilling to let her walk on her wounded leg. "I've seen some of the worst things in life with the Coast Guard. With you, I'll get to see some of the best."

She truly hoped so. No…she vowed to make sure that happened, so that neither one of them got too sucked into their careers.

"And as for my professional take on our chances as a couple?" She wrapped her arms around his neck as he cradled her tight against him.

"Yeah?" He kicked the door closed, ready to stride into his future with this incredible woman at his side.

"I'd say we're the odds-on favorites to make it work."

* * * * *

*Celebrate 60 years of
pure reading pleasure with Harlequin®!
Silhouette® Romantic Suspense is celebrating
with the glamour-filled, adrenaline-charged series
LOVE IN 60 SECONDS
starting in April 2009.
Six stories that promise to bring
the glitz of Las Vegas, the danger of revenge,
the mystery of a missing diamond, family scandals
and ripped-from-the-headlines intrigue.
Get your heart racing as
love happens in sixty seconds!*

*Enjoy a sneak peek of
USA TODAY bestselling author
Marie Ferrarella's
THE HEIRESS'S 2-WEEK AFFAIR
Available April 2009
from Silhouette® Romantic Suspense.*

Eight years ago Matt Shaffer had vanished out of Natalie Rothchild's life, leaving behind a one-line note tucked under a pillow that had grown cold: *I'm sorry, but this just isn't going to work.*

That was it. No explanation, no real indication of remorse. The note had been as clinical and compassionless as an eviction notice, which, in effect, it had been, Natalie thought as she navigated through the morning traffic. Matt had written the note to evict her from his life.

She'd spent the next two weeks crying, breaking down without warning as she walked down the street, or as she sat staring at a meal she couldn't bring herself to eat.

Candace, she remembered with a bittersweet pang, had tried to get her to go clubbing in order to get her to forget about Matt.

She'd turned her twin down, but she did get her act

together. If Matt didn't think enough of their relationship to try to contact her, to try to make her understand why he'd changed so radically from lover to stranger, then to hell with him. He was dead to her, she resolved. And he'd remained that way.

Until twenty minutes ago.

The adrenaline in her veins kept mounting.

Natalie focused on her driving. Vegas in the daylight wasn't nearly as alluring, as magical and glitzy as it was after dark. Like an aging woman best seen in soft lighting, Vegas's imperfections were all visible in the daylight. Natalie supposed that was why people like her sister didn't like to get up until noon. They lived for the night.

Except that Candace could no longer do that.

The thought brought a fresh, sharp ache with it.

"Damn it, Candy, what a waste," Natalie murmured under her breath.

She pulled up before the Janus casino. One of the three valets currently on duty came to life and made a beeline for her vehicle.

"Welcome to the Janus," the young attendant said cheerfully as he opened her door with a flourish.

"We'll see," she replied solemnly.

As he pulled away with her car, Natalie looked up at the casino's logo. Janus was the Roman god with two faces, one pointed toward the past, the other facing the future. It struck her as rather ironic, given what she was doing here, seeking out someone from her past in order to get answers so that the future could be settled.

The moment she entered the casino, the Vegas phenomena took hold. It was like stepping into a world where time did not matter or even make an appearance. There was only a sense of "now."

Because in Natalie's experience she'd discovered that bartenders knew the inner workings of any establishment they worked for better than anyone else, she made her way to the first bar she saw within the casino.

The bartender in attendance was a gregarious man in his early forties. He had a quick, sexy smile, which was probably one of the main reasons he'd been hired. His name tag identified him as Kevin.

Moving to her end of the bar, Kevin asked, "What'll it be, pretty lady?"

"Information." She saw a dubious look cross his brow. To counter that, she took out her badge. Granted she wasn't here in an official capacity, but Kevin didn't need to know that. "Were you on duty last night?"

Kevin began to wipe the gleaming black surface of the bar. "You mean during the gala?"

"Yes."

The smile gracing his lips was a satisfied one. Last night had obviously been profitable for him, she judged. "I caught an extra shift."

She took out Candace's photograph and carefully placed it on the bar. "Did you happen to see this woman there?"

The bartender glanced at the picture. Mild interest turned to recognition. "You mean Candace Rothchild? Yeah, she was here, loud and brassy as always. But not for long," he added, looking rather disappointed. There was always a circus when Candace was around, Natalie thought. "She and the boss had at it and then he had our head of security escort her out."

She latched onto the first part of his statement. "They argued? About what?"

He shook his head. "Couldn't tell you. Too far away for anything but body language," he confessed.

"And the head of security?" she asked.

"He got her to leave."

She leaned in over the bar. "Tell me about him."

"Don't know much," the bartender admitted. "Just that his name's Matt Shaffer. Boss flew him in from L.A., where he was head of security for Montgomery Enterprises."

There was no avoiding it, she thought darkly. She was going to have to talk to Matt. The thought left her cold. "Do you know where I can find him right now?"

Kevin glanced at his watch. "He should be in his office. On the second floor, toward the rear." He gave her the numbers of the rooms where the monitors that kept watch over the casino guests as they tried their luck against the house were located.

Taking out a twenty, she placed it on the bar. "Thanks for your help."

Kevin slipped the bill into his vest pocket. "Any time, lovely lady," he called after her. "Any time."

She debated going up the stairs, then decided on the elevator. The car that took her up to the second floor was empty. Natalie stepped out of the elevator, looked around to get her bearings and then walked toward the rear of the floor.

"Into the Valley of Death rode the six hundred," she silently recited, digging deep for a line from a poem by Tennyson. Wrapping her hand around a brass handle, she opened one of the glass doors and walked in.

The woman whose desk was closest to the door looked up. "You can't come in here. This is a restricted area."

Natalie already had her ID in her hand and held it up. "I'm looking for Matt Shaffer," she told the woman.

God, even saying his name made her mouth go dry. She was supposed to be over him, to have moved on with her life. What happened?

The woman began to answer her. "He's—"

"Right here."

The deep voice came from behind her. Natalie felt every single nerve ending go on tactical alert at the same moment that all the hairs at the back of her neck stood up. Eight years had passed, but she would have recognized his voice anywhere.

* * * * *

Why did Matt Shaffer leave
heiress-turned-cop Natalie Rothchild?
What does he know about the death
of Natalie's twin sister?
Come and meet these two reunited lovers and
learn the secrets of the Rothchild family in
THE HEIRESS'S 2-WEEK AFFAIR
by USA TODAY bestselling author
Marie Ferrarella.
The first book in
Silhouette® Romantic Suspense's
wildly romantic new continuity,
LOVE IN 60 SECONDS!
Available April 2009.

Harlequin® Historical
Historical Romantic Adventure!

Undone!

THE RAKE'S INHERITED COURTESAN
Ann Lethbridge

Christopher Evernden has been
assigned the unfortunate task of minding
Parisian courtesan Sylvia Boisette.
When Syliva sets off to find her father,
Christopher has no choice but to follow
and finds her kidnapped by an Irishman.
Once rescued, they finally succumb to
the temptation that has been brewing
between them. But can they see past the
limitations such a love can bring?

Available April 2009
wherever books are sold.

You're invited to join our Tell Harlequin Reader Panel!

By joining our new reader panel you will:

- Receive Harlequin® books—they are FREE and yours to keep with no obligation to purchase anything!
- Participate in fun online surveys
- Exchange opinions and ideas with women just like you
- Have a say in our new book ideas and help us publish the best in women's fiction

In addition, you will have a chance to win great prizes and receive special gifts! See Web site for details. Some conditions apply. Space is limited.

To join, visit us at
www.TellHarlequin.com.

The Inside Romance newsletter has a NEW look for the new year!

Same great content, brand-new look!

The Inside Romance newsletter is a FREE quarterly newsletter highlighting our upcoming series releases and promotions!

Click on the Inside Romance link on the front page of **www.eHarlequin.com** or e-mail us at insideromance@harlequin.ca to sign up to receive your FREE newsletter today!

You can also subscribe by writing to us at: HARLEQUIN BOOKS Attention: Customer Service Department P.O. Box 9057, Buffalo, NY 14269-9057

Please allow 4-6 weeks for delivery of the first issue by mail.

IRNNEW09

REQUEST YOUR FREE BOOKS!

2 FREE NOVELS
PLUS 2
FREE GIFTS!

HARLEQUIN®

Blaze™

Red-hot reads!

YES! Please send me 2 FREE Harlequin® Blaze™ novels and my 2 FREE gifts (gifts are worth about $10). After receiving them, if I don't wish to receive any more books, I can return the shipping statement marked "cancel". If I don't cancel, I will receive 6 brand-new novels every month and be billed just $4.24 per book in the U.S. or $4.71 per book in Canada. Shipping and handling is just 25¢ per book. That's a savings of 15% or more off the cover price! I understand that accepting the 2 free books and gifts places me under no obligation to buy anything. I can always return a shipment and cancel at any time. Even if I never buy another book, the two free books and gifts are mine to keep forever.

151 HDN ERVA 351 HDN ERUX

Name	(PLEASE PRINT)	
Address		Apt. #
City	State/Prov.	Zip/Postal Code

Signature (if under 18, a parent or guardian must sign)

Mail to the Harlequin Reader Service:
IN U.S.A.: P.O. Box 1867, Buffalo, NY 14240-1867
IN CANADA: P.O. Box 609, Fort Erie, Ontario L2A 5X3

Not valid to current subscribers of Harlequin Blaze books.

Want to try two free books from another line?
Call 1-800-873-8635 or visit www.morefreebooks.com.

* Terms and prices subject to change without notice. Prices do not include applicable taxes. N.Y. residents add applicable sales tax. Canadian residents will be charged applicable provincial taxes and GST. Offer not valid in Quebec. This offer is limited to one order per household. All orders subject to approval. Credit or debit balances in a customer's account(s) may be offset by any other outstanding balance owed by or to the customer. Please allow 4 to 6 weeks for delivery. Offer available while quantities last.

Your Privacy: Harlequin Books is committed to protecting your privacy. Our Privacy Policy is available online at www.eHarlequin.com or upon request from the Reader Service. From time to time we make our lists of customers available to reputable third parties who may have a product or service of interest to you. If you would prefer we not share your name and address, please check here. ☐

HB09R

HARLEQUIN® *Blaze*™

Two delightfully sexy stories.
Two determined, free-spirited heroines
and two irresistible heroes...
who won't have a clue what hit them!

Don't miss
TAWNY WEBER'S
first duet:

Coming On Strong
April 2009

and

Going Down Hard
May 2009

The spring is turning out to be a hot one!

Available wherever Harlequin books are sold.

www.eHarlequin.com

COMING NEXT MONTH
Available March 31, 2009

#459 OUT OF CONTROL Julie Miller
From 0–60
Detective Jack Riley is determined to uncover who's behind the movement
of drugs through Dahlia Speedway. And he'll do whatever it takes to find out—
even go undercover as a driver. But can he keep his hands off sexy mechanic
Alex Morgan?

#460 NAKED ATTRACTION Jule McBride
Robby Robriquet's breathtaking looks and chiseled bod just can't be denied.
But complications ensue for Ellie Lee and Robby when his dad wants Ellie's
business skills for a sneaky scheme that jeopardizes their love all over again….

#461 ONCE A GAMBLER Carrie Hudson
Stolen from Time, Bk. 2
Riverboat gambler Jake Gannon's runnin', cheatin' ways may have come to
an end when he aids the sweet Ellie Winslow in her search for her sister. Ellie
claims she's been sent back in time, but Jake's bettin' he'll be able to convince
her to stay!

#462 COMING ON STRONG Tawny Weber
Paybacks can be hell. That's what Belle Forsham finds out when she looks
up former fiancé Mitch Carter. So she left him at the altar six years ago? But
she needs his help now. What else can she do but show him what he's been
missing?

#463 THE RIGHT STUFF Lori Wilde
Uniformly Hot!
Taylor Milton is researching her next planned fantasy adventure resort—Out of
This World Lovemaking—featuring sexy air force high fliers. Volunteering for
duty is Lieutenant Colonel Dr. Daniel Corben, who's ready and able to take the
glam heiress to the moon and back!

#464 SHE'S GOT IT BAD Sarah Mayberry
Zoe Ford can't believe that Liam Masters has walked into her tattoo parlor. After
all this time he's still an irresistible bad boy. But she's no longer sweet and
innocent. And she has a score to settle with him. One that won't be paid until
he's hot, bothered and begging for more.

HBCNMBPA0309